ABOUT THIS BOOK

Welcome to the darker, sexier side of Havenwood Falls that many residents never speak of publicly, but most likely enjoy in secret. Venture into the SIN MC, the VIP rooms of Silk nightclub, and behind other closed doors, where you'll discover passion, unusual penchants, and just how far some will go for love. Hold on to your panties, because it's time to ride . . .

After being gone for several decades, Gabriel Doyle feels drawn to his former hometown in Colorado. His memories are vague and blurry, but he can't resist the urge to go, especially when the woman in his dreams begins to appear in real life. What he's not so sure about is what he faces on his return—leading the Lilith Nest vampires.

Needing a fresh start, Alina Anand takes a nanny job for a mage family in Havenwood Falls. At first, life is great. She loves her charges and finds the town quaint and welcoming, but everything changes when her employers steal her amulet—and take control of her wish-granting powers. Bound to them by tradition, she has no choice but to serve them.

When their destinies collide, Gabriel and Alina discover a connection that goes beyond their undeniable passion. But to save Alina, Gabriel must decide whether to pick up the dark life of bloodshed and revenge he left behind, or to ask for help from those who demand sacrifice. Nothing in life is free. The star-crossed lovers must fight for what they desire most—to be who they are, love who they want, and escape the bonds of their pasts in a town that forgives little and forgets nothing.

HAVENWOOD FALLS SIN & SILK BOOKS

Taming the Beast by Nadirah Foxx

Plans Laid Bare by JD Nelson

Shift of Fate by Victoria Escobar

Stolen Wishes by Victoria Flynn

Damned Allure by Justine Winter

Savage Salvation by Kristie Cook

Dark Seduction by Michele G. Miller & R.K. Ryals

Soul Laid Bare by JD Nelson

Stray With Me by E.J. Fechenda

Chase the Flames by Desiree Lafawn

Flirting With Death by Nadirah Foxx

Also try the signature line, Havenwood Falls, the historical paranormal line, Legends of Havenwood Falls, and stories from the local supernatural college in Sun & Moon Academy.

Stay up to date at www.HavenwoodFalls.com

ALSO BY VICTORIA FLYNN

STOLEN WISHES

A HAVENWOOD FALLS SIN & SILK NOVELLA

VICTORIA FLYNN

For Love and Lust. May the two forever enhance the spice of life.

PROLOGUE

GABRIEL

*H*er skin was smooth and flawless like Chinese porcelain, and the way her heart drummed excitedly in her chest when I touched her drove me wild. She was a drug I was hopelessly addicted to.

"I've missed you," she whispered, dropping the sheet she had wrapped around herself.

The scent of her arousal invaded my senses and blurred any clear thoughts. All-consuming, that was what the vixen was to me.

Tugging my shirt over my head and throwing it to the ground, I strode toward my prize. Her nipples were drawn up into tight buds as I crossed the expanse of my hotel suite to her. Oh yes, she wanted me. She rubbed her thighs together as if it could relieve the pressure of her desire.

"You're all I can think about. Even when I'm awake, I feel like I'm just passing the time until you're in my arms again," I confessed.

My nameless beauty closed the gap between us, nipping the tender flesh over my collar bone and sliding down me, sinking to her knees. Her hands worked quickly to free me from my slacks. My cock sprung free and her eyes devoured every inch. Her pink tongue swept over her lips, and her eyes dared me to deny her what she wanted.

"Hungry?" I teased, stepping out of my pants and fisting my throbbing cock.

She nodded slowly, leaning forward until her breath fanned over me, making me damn near lose control on the spot. Her fingers skimmed over my sensitive skin before wrapping around me securely. Her hand slid up and down my length lazily, and I let my eyes fall closed, relishing every second. Her hot, slick tongue traced the thick shaft from the bottom up, and her lips enveloped me as she reached the top.

"Fuck," I groaned, my hips flexing instinctively and driving me deeper into her mouth.

I could feel the muscles of her mouth stretch into a coy smile just before she set about her task, taking me in as deeply as she could. Pressure was growing low in my belly, and every nerve was firing like a Fourth of July display. Picking up the pace, her head bobbed up and down as she pushed me faster toward my peak. Her deft fingers worked furiously between her legs. It was a sight that would drive a lesser man to his knees with need, but she was mine, only mine, to savor.

She repeated the same pattern, taking me in deep and then flicking her succulent tongue over the head of my dick. The woman was driving me wild and playing me like a well-loved instrument. Her free hand snaked down, cupping my balls and dragging her nails over them, bringing me to my tipping point.

"Christ, you need to stop, or I'm going to come," I warned her, holding back and giving her plenty of time to release her hold, but she didn't.

Her devious eyes darted to my own, dancing with mirth as she sucked harder. I was a goner under her skilled touch. Not two minutes later, thick ropes of cum erupted from me, coating her throat as I roared in ecstasy. The vixen swallowed down every drop like she was starved for it, drawing it out until my last spasm faded.

She licked her lips with satisfaction, her heavy-lidded eyes betraying her arousal.

"I want more."

Drained of energy, I crossed to the bed and held my hand out to her. Just before she came close enough, the room faded to black, and she was torn away from me.

My eyes cracked open before I could reach her. The room was dark, but I could tell the sun was beginning to set. It was another dream.

Every day for months, the bronzed goddess had visited me and drawn me into her thrall. Women had thrown themselves at me, yet the nameless woman from my dreams had been all I could think about. Hell, my dick wouldn't even respond to another anymore, not of its own volition anyway. My cock was painfully hard, and my fangs dug into my lower lip with my desire, despite the exotic woman's absence.

I could still see her stunning figure standing before me as vividly as though it had just happened, begging me to come for her. Her sensuous voice called to me, telling me she was waiting for me in Havenwood Falls, and I couldn't live on dreams anymore. I had to know if she was real, no matter what.

CHAPTER 1

GABRIEL

*T*here it was again. The relentless pull to leave. This time was different, though. This time, it whispered a name I'd heard before . . . in my dreams. My recurring vision came back to me. An exotic beauty and somewhere called Havenwood Falls. The name had been repeated until it was all I could think about. When I'd done a search, nothing had shown up. I decided to make some calls. Eventually, I'd been able to narrow it down to the mountains of Colorado. No one could remember the town, nor its location, but I'd been told at least twice that I should check out the majestic mountains of the western state. With the red-eye tickets booked, I gave my thoughts back to the beauty who'd been haunting me. I could still picture her sensual form standing before me in my Paris hotel room, whispering for me to come to her in the mysterious town. She was waiting for me.

In the many nights we'd shared, never had I learned her name. It tormented me incessantly. When I ventured out into the city, it never failed that I'd catch a glimpse of a woman who shared some feature with the woman I'd come to care for—long black hair like a raven's feather, a rich tan, eyes like a smooth cognac. Those women were never her.

I pushed the thoughts away, not wanting to obsess over the identity of the mystery woman more than I already had. Swirling my whiskey around the tumbler, I stood on my suite's balcony overlooking Montmartre.

Paris had grown gray with the late autumn season. Rain drizzled down on the city, and I found I wasn't sad to be leaving. When you lived as long as I had, cities like London, Rome, Paris, and Prague lost their luster.

Home.

It was an odd thought. The closest thing I'd ever had to a home had been with my closest friend and sire, Viktor. He'd settled somewhere in Colorado and started a small empire for himself.

He was gone now, which had been a large part of why I'd stayed away from America as long as I had. Would home still be home if the person who made it special was no longer there? That was still to be seen.

"Lorenzo!" I called out, striding into the parlor and abandoning the balcony overlooking the narrow streets of France.

"What can I do for you, sir?" the small Italian man chirped, appearing almost out of nowhere.

"You may let the staff know we will be departing for America in the coming week. Have you ever been to Colorado, Enzo?" I asked, loosening my tie.

"No, sir. This will be my first trip." His thick Italian accent was barely comprehensible. "I hope you'll let me know what to expect and what I should pack for."

"It's late autumn. The Colorado mountains are cold, damp, and could be snow-covered. Layers, my friend."

"*Grazie*, sir. I will make the necessary arrangements. May I ask why the sudden change in plans? I was under the impression we'd be staying in Paris until the end of January before continuing on to Amsterdam."

Lorenzo was good people and the only person I fully trusted. He was nearly forty and had been in my service since he'd reached adulthood. As a blood servant went, he was top notch, and as a friend, he was one of my closest. His family had served me since Viktor had raised me out of the gutter and turned me into a proper gentleman over three centuries earlier. Blend in, watch, find a weakness, and exploit it—those had been my first lessons. I'd done that when I'd stumbled across Alessio De Luca, Lorenzo's seventh great grandfather. He'd been able to do something I'd thought was lost to me since becoming a vampire: he could make me laugh. Instead of killing the poor bastard, I'd offered him a job. The rest, as they say, was history.

"It's hard to explain. I've always been a nomad. However, there's something different about Colorado. It's the closest thing I've ever had to a home, even more than Ireland," I joked, letting my natural brogue slip back into my words.

"How long?" Enzo asked, concern written in the shallow creases beginning to form from age.

Despite being a few hundred years younger than me, Lorenzo looked older than my frozen twenty-eight years.

"I haven't been home in more than forty years. Not since before Viktor passed," I answered, ignoring the pangs of loss that could still send me reeling, if I let them.

"Understandable, sir. He was a father to you, and that sort of grief is felt for a lifetime," he replied.

He was right. I knew Viktor was gone, but going home without his warm welcome would be difficult. That was the thing about vampires—we'd grieve a loss for centuries, because time no longer mattered. Things were felt on a deeper level because such things are fleeting.

"I suppose you're right, but there are other matters to tackle while on this trip," I answered, and there were.

Being a vampire came with its constraints, like not being able to walk in the daylight, but it also gave those like me ample time to grow a fortune. Unlike some, I'd grown with the times, seeing no point in dwelling on the inventions and ideals of the past. When the internet had come along, I'd invested, knowing that it would somehow change the future of the modern world. Then had come the capability to conduct such investments online, and I never needed to work again. When you've been around longer than the stock market itself, you pick up a thing or two about money, stock trends, and good investments. Having spent the better part of two centuries building a fortune, I was now in a position to make moves and flex my muscles. Everyone, regardless of species, could recognize that money was power, and whoever had the most made the rules of how the rest played the game.

"I'm sorry, Gabriel. I don't follow," Enzo said.

I frowned slightly, realizing I hadn't mentioned the dreams or the side trip.

"I apologize, old friend. Things have been difficult. These dreams I've been having . . . I've never experienced anything like them. Actually, I don't believe I remember ever dreaming until a few months ago."

"Would you like me to search the archives? Perhaps there could be an answer there as to what this means?"

I nodded. "Sure. Thank you, Lorenzo. That would be helpful, though my point was that in these dreams, a voice keeps saying *Havenwood Falls*. I think it's in Colorado, near Viktor's old home. I need to know if there's something to all of this there."

"I understand. I'll make the necessary preparations. In the meantime, you haven't fed in a few days," he stated, undoing the button holding his sleeve together.

"I've already booked our flights, but other transportation will need to be arranged."

Enzo pushed his sleeve up, exposing his arm to me. He sat on the sofa, leaving room for me to join him. A pinch in my gums was all I needed to know my fangs had extended, ready to feed. The tight hold I kept on the monster inside me slipped a little, and I pounced on Lorenzo's offering. My fangs tore through his flesh like a hot knife through butter. His blood was like cinnamon and cloves, spicy and aromatic. I drank until the beast inside me was sated and released before I'd taken too much. Like the professional he was, Enzo produced a small hanky and wiped the crimson smear at the edge of my mouth before wrapping his wound tightly. He rose a little unsteadily, my only indication that I'd gotten a little carried away this time. With a quick bow, Lorenzo turned and exited the room.

Shame coursed through me.

There was a time I wouldn't have felt anything for those I'd fed from. Anyone who was unlucky enough to cross my path was lower than me on the food chain; it was natural. That's what I'd told myself for years. Hell, I'd lived for the hunt. The feeling when life finally left someone and the light faded from their eyes had been a drug to me. Viktor and I had even gone to war on several occasions, making a game of killing our foes in the most imaginative way possible. Grown men had fallen in shreds at my feet. Then one day, all of that changed.

I couldn't put a finger on what had been the turning point for me, but after almost a century of living in a constant bloodbath, I'd found myself wanting more. Viktor was calculating. One always had to be on their toes around him. He'd taught me a lot, yet there no longer seemed to be a point to life without someone to share it with, on a different level. I wanted to watch art be born from a beautiful mind and bright thinkers rise to the famed pages of history. I wanted to experience it all as a free man.

As a mortal, I'd been nothing more than a slave. Despite the practice being considered illegal, I'd been taken after the soldiers slaughtered my mother at the Siege of Galway, when King Charles II's men came to topple Catholicism in Ireland. My father had succumbed to the pox a year earlier, along with my little sister, Mary. In my twenty-eight years as a human, I'd never known what it was to do as I pleased. As a vampire, I was desperate for a taste of freedom.

My change of heart had driven a wedge between Viktor and me, but eventually, he came to understand that I needed more than he could give me. Like a baby bird, I had reached the time to leave the nest and spread my wings. So, I did.

In my arrogance and stubbornness, I'd lost almost thirty years with my sire. He'd been gone more than ten years now, lost to the insanity

9

that came with drinking drug-tainted blood. I couldn't help feeling responsible for it. If I had been there, would things have gone differently for him? I'd spent far too long running away from my past, and it was time to go home. It was time to say my final goodbyes to Viktor Azimov, my father and sire, and it was time to look to the future and the mysteries that Havenwood Falls would offer.

CHAPTER 2

ALINA

*D*addy was going to be pissed. Anands stuck together and never ventured too far from the family. Family was protection, and to Daddy, that was everything. Me getting a job hours away from home wouldn't be acceptable, but at twenty-four, it was necessary if I was to keep any of my sanity or sense of self.

I glanced at the scribbled details on the front page of my open notebook.

Havenwood Falls.

I'd never heard of it before, and no matter how many times I'd put the town into my GPS, I still came up with nothing. It was worrying. Was it so small that it didn't show up on maps?

"Do you really have to go? Things won't be the same with you gone," my younger sister, Kalene, whined from where she sat in my computer chair.

"I know, but this is something I have to do. If it doesn't work out, then fine, I can always come back home. What if it does work out though? I could have that life I've always dreamed of, a place of my own where I make my own rules, my own life. Besides, you're getting a little old to need someone to cover for your antics."

"I know, but where's the fun in that? You have to promise me that you'll still come home to visit sometimes, and after you're settled, I'll come up for a weekend. Who knows, maybe I'll fall in love with Hardwood Springs and never leave," she teased.

"Havenwood Falls. Hardwood Springs? Where did you pull that from?" I chuckled, throwing the last of my toiletries into my bag.

"Ehh, potato, potahto," she shrugged.

Kalene was only a year younger than I was, but was easily still eighteen mentally. She wasn't the type to take much seriously, but it was what I loved about her.

"All right, it's a deal. I promise to come home, and as long as it's allowed, you're welcome to come stay with me when you need to get out of here for a while."

I slid the zipper closed and moved to sit on the bed next to her. Kalene threw her arm over my shoulders and leaned in. This was going to be the last time we sat on my bed together. I'd miss her horribly, but there were absolutely zero doubts in my mind that I was doing the right thing. Space and the chance to make something for myself without my father dictating what my duties were would only ever be possible if I left.

The clock on the wall chimed. It was time to go. If I didn't get on the road, I'd miss the bus to the place where I was laying down roots—Havenwood Falls.

I bid my family who would still speak to me farewell; my father was not among them. My mother said he'd come around, and they'd come to visit me, but the rift in the family was being felt by everyone. My older brother had yet to speak to me since I'd announced I was leaving. Of my three siblings, Kalene was the only one who got it. She understood my need to leave, to be free to live my life the way I wanted to and not by what my parents told me I had to do. If they couldn't cut the cord, then I would. That's what I reminded myself of as my car pulled away from the only home I'd ever known. I was closing the door on one part of my life and turning the page to begin something new; the thrill of not knowing what lay ahead was intoxicating.

Kalene drove me to the bus station, bidding me a teary farewell and promising to come visit after Christmas. Despite the sorrow I was feeling, I couldn't hide my excitement. I was practically bouncing in my seat. When the bus finally pulled up, I almost sprinted for the open door, ready to begin this new adventure.

I climbed on board and found a seat near the back of the bus. Pulling my jacket tighter around me, I put my hood up and dug out my ear phones, flipping to my favorite radio station on my phone. Ducking my face, I tried to make myself invisible as another twenty or so people filed their way onto the bus and into seats. Luckily, no one decided to occupy the one directly next to mine.

It wasn't that I didn't like people—I did—but I'd been burned by false niceties and so-called friends too many times to go out of my way to create more relationships. So I kept to myself and liked it that way. When my cousin, Malia, sent me the job listing and it wasn't something where I'd have to put on a fake smile, I'd nearly teleported to the town on the spot. As luck would have it, the Grandvilles—a prestigious old English family familiar with the ways of magic—had hired me after only a brief telephone interview. The parameters were set in stone, and there was no doubt where I stood with these people. I'd do my job and care for their children, and they'd pay me enough to finance a life of my own. All I had to do was relax and enjoy the ride.

I closed my eyes and let the landscape pass by as the journey got underway. Soulful country ballads about love and heartbreak lulled me into a near sleep-like state, aided by the swaying motion of the bus. Somewhere along the way, not too long into the trip, I drifted off to sleep.

A cool breeze caressed my bare skin. Glancing down, I realized I was wearing a sand-colored sheer dress and not much more than that. My hair fell in curls down my back.

"I almost thought you weren't coming," a deep masculine voice said from behind me.

His words were heavy with an Irish brogue that turned my insides molten. Bright blue eyes greeted mine, crinkled with a warm smile.

"Where are we?" I asked, turning to take in the room.

A massive four-poster bed sat against the innermost wall, draped in white muslin and red silk. I squeezed my thighs together to stave off the desire that had ignited within me.

His arms circled around my waist as he pulled me back against his solid chest. My ass pressed back against the hard ridge that tented his slacks. As if by instinct, I wanted to submit and open myself up to this stranger, but was he really a stranger? The way he spoke to me and touched me made me think we'd known each other for years.

"Paris, for now," he whispered, before his lips latched onto my ear lobe.

My breath hitched, and my knees threatened to buckle under his expert touch. His ravenous lips trailed down to the junction of my neck and shoulder, placing a tender kiss there. Reaching back, my fingers threaded through his thick brown hair, tugging just enough to spur him on. Dragging me against the hard planes of his body, he lifted my skirt and his hand disappeared as he inched closer to my aching core.

The squealing of brakes jolted me out of my slumber just when things were getting good. It was another dream, and I wanted to kick myself for enjoying it as much as I had. No man had ever touched me with such passion as *he* had. He'd been working me into a frenzy several nights a week, always remaining a mystery. I'd agonized over his identity, praying he was real and would find his way to me, to no avail. I doubted a real man ever would ravage me the way I craved when I was with him. Those weren't the sort of men my father wanted for me, anyway.

Rubbing the sleep from my eyes, I glanced out the window, but couldn't get a good look at the town. The sun had long since gone down, and the moon was nearly nonexistent, making the night sky darker than I was used to in Denver. Street lights shone brightly on the little town that would be my new home.

The bus rolled to a stop. One by one, we filed down the narrow aisle and out onto the cold street. The bus driver was busy pulling suitcases from the storage compartment and piling them in a heap behind him. He didn't stick around too long. By the time I had my fingers wrapped around the handle of my bag, he had the bus doors shut and was shifting into gear.

"See ya, wouldn't wanna be ya," I murmured under my breath.

The crowd around me was quickly dispersing to their individual locations. People spread in every direction around the town square, disappearing before I could ask anyone if they knew where I was supposed to go.

The only thing I had to go on was an address. Strangely, no matter how many times I tried to pull up the map app on my phone, it couldn't or wouldn't get a read on where I was. It was useless. The only directions I had were that the home was in someplace called Creekwood, and it was off the main drag into town. When I pulled up the compass app, the needle just swung around aimlessly.

Strange.

If I could get away with it, I would use my magic to zap my butt right on over to the address on the paper, but I couldn't risk anyone seeing me. I'd never dared to use it outside the privacy of home before, and I wasn't about to start in an unfamiliar place.

"Never let anyone see your magic. It's special, my little Lina, and always keep your opal safe." My father's words replayed in my head, the same as they did every time I wanted to use my powers outside.

Too risky.

Glancing around the town square, I spied a woman closing up shop for the night. Not wasting any time, I quickly headed straight for her. Pride went right out the window when it came to being lost.

"Excuse me?" I called out, hurrying over to her.

The woman cast a quick glance over her shoulder, seeming surprised that I was addressing her.

"Yes?" she said.

"Hi! Sorry, I'm new here, just arrived actually, and I was hoping you could tell me where to find somewhere called Creekwood? Here's the address," I explained, handing over the small piece of paper with my destination scribbled on it. "Gosh, I'm sorry. Where are my manners? My name's Alina Anand."

"Hannah Pederson. Nice to meet you," she answered, extending her hand to me.

As I shook her hand, she quickly grabbed the paper and scanned over its contents. While she was reading, I looked her over a little closer. Hannah's hair was short and wild with rich fiery high- and lowlights throughout. She was petite and utterly adorable, the sort of woman that could make anyone at ease with just her presence.

"Okay, so this is just up the road that way. Right when you come into town on County Road 13, it's to the left. Look for Blackstone Road, it splits from the County Road, and Creekwood's right there, can't miss it."

"Thank you so much!" I replied, waving farewell.

Putting one foot in front of the other, I began the short walk to Creekwood. The moon was barely a sliver, casting long shadows along the valley. Mountains towered over the town, boxing it in on all sides. The night air was cold, and snow coated the ground. I pulled my coat tighter around me and kept my quick pace. Something was unsettling about my new home. The town was . . . different. Though I couldn't quite put my finger on what was off. Toeing the line between being afraid and having enough confidence in my magic to defend myself, I kept a close eye on the darkness between lampposts. It was the sort of darkness that put you on edge and made you feel like you were being watched from just beyond the borders of the lights. I may have been a Marid djinn, but I wasn't naïve enough to think I was the baddest being out there. There were things that would give even my kind nightmares.

Djinn like me had a long history of falling prey to more powerful beings. The legend was that we descended from Set, who grew jealous of Amani and Khalida, the djinn twins created by Sekhmet and Shu. He thought he could replicate them and set out to do just that. Eventually, the Marid line was born.

The wish granters.

Our power was rooted in the elements we were born from and only a fraction of the god's power, but it was enough. Each individual had his or her own strength, be it brewing up snow for a white

Christmas or conjuring a chest full of precious gems. All Marids could step between planes of existence, making travel rather convenient, as we could teleport anywhere we wanted or make a fast escape. However, there were limits. We couldn't change someone's heart or bring back the dead, much to the dismay of some.

We could make someone's dreams come true, their every desire, and that's why they wanted us so badly. If you had control of a being who could make your fantasy a reality, you'd be the most powerful person in the world. Some Marids became cocky, too loose with their magic. So we'd been cursed, each of our souls and our sources of power tied to a special object, one we must keep safe at all costs. It was a safeguard of sorts. It could be our prison or grant our freedom, because without the object, no one could force us to do anything.

My fingers went to the opal necklace set into a gold floral filigree setting hanging down between my breasts. It was still there, a stark reminder of what I had to lose. No one could know about the necklace.

When I'd first been contacted by the Grandvilles, they'd been very upfront about needing someone with certain *capabilities* to help with the children. They didn't want just any paranormal being. They wanted someone who could handle a fledgling witch. When asked what type of being I was, I had been reticent to answer truthfully, although my cousin, Malia, was known for having loose lips and had readily told the woman what I was. When Mrs. Grandville admitted to already knowing my lineage, she mentioned wanting to know how forthcoming I was with sensitive information. The family was very private, homeschooling the children and keeping to themselves as often as possible. My own family had been the same way, albeit for different reasons. My kind were fairly rare, having been hunted to the brink of extinction. That information could easily put a target on my back.

I'd left home because my father and family were stifling me, beyond overbearing. They were always reminding me how unsafe it was to live alone, out in the world, but it was all I'd ever wanted. A job to support myself, traveling the world, meeting new people—all of it had been my dream since I was small, and the reality was now within reach. If I had stayed at home, my father would have found me a suitable match and expected me to settle down and make more djinn babies, as he thought was my lot in life. He'd never really taken the opportunity to get to know me. If he had, he'd have known I'd never go along with something like that. I was headstrong, like him.

The street lamp overhead flickered. I quickened my pace, seeing the neighborhood come into view. So what if I was a magical being? The dark still creeped me out when I was alone and made me feel like a helpless child again. The only difference was now as an adult, I knew what lurked in the dark, and it was every bit as terrifying as I'd thought.

I passed into the neighborhood, eyeing the houses as best as I could. Most were lit up; it was still early, only six thirty, and families were settling down for dinner. The homes were nice—nothing too extravagant, yet clearly upscale and well maintained. Digging into my pockets, I searched for the paper with the address, realizing that I could've already passed it, as I was lost in my thoughts.

259 Flynn Court.

There was a cross street ahead, the street sign lit by the light overhead.

Flynn Court.

I was in the right place, then. I moved quickly, noting the odd numbers were on the left. Passing house after house without finding my destination, I began to worry the house didn't exist. Was it all some elaborate prank? Would some college kid jump out with a camera at any moment?

There was a single house left on the street. It had to be the one I was looking for. Shrubs grew up around the cement front porch, creating a sort of fence that obscured most of the lower level of the home. The two-story brick house sported large windows, flanked by black shutters, and mostly closed off by curtains. A mature rowan tree stood in the center of the front yard. I couldn't make out the numbers on the house from the road, so I ventured closer.

The numbers were hidden by the shrubs, however as I got closer, I could make out the 259 more clearly. I was finally in the right place. Climbing the stairs, I placed myself square with the door and hesitated before knocking. A million things that could go wrong stampeded through my thoughts.

Taking one last deep breath, I rapped my knuckles against the wooden door. I stepped back, not wanting to seem overbearing. I heard the distinct click of heels on a hard surface before a shadow appeared on the other side of the door through the frosted window. The door swung in, and a woman no more than thirty-five stood in its entrance. Her face was slim, angular, and austere, with an upturned button nose. Her light brown hair was waved to perfection. Her pouty mouth turned down in a frown as she took me in.

"Hi! My name's Alina Anand, and I believe I have the right address. Are you Mrs. Grandville?" I asked, extending my hand forth.

CHAPTER 3

ALINA

*H*er nose scrunched in disgust as she stared at my hand and then up at my face again.

"So, you're the genie," she surmised, appraising me.

Well, this is certainly not what I was expecting, I thought to myself.

"Djinn. Yes, ma'am, I am. You can just call me Alina." I tried to keep my calm as she looked down her nose at me.

"I'm Edith Grandville, but you will address me by Mrs. Grandville. Am I clear?"

I nodded quickly, not wanting to make a crap first impression. My magic prickled under my skin, being so near to another powerful being. I wondered briefly if she felt it, too, though I didn't have the courage to ask.

Is she always so formal and uptight? I wondered, despite my gut saying yes. She stepped aside, tipping her head to invite me in. I passed into her home and immediately noted the house was practically a museum. Nothing looked used or out of place, and every surface was spotless.

Mrs. Grandville moved around me and came to a stop, blocking my path farther into the house. With a flick of her hand, the door closed securely behind me. Her hand gave a sharp twist, and I could hear the metallic sound of the lock being turned. My eyes widened. I had known the Grandvilles were magical, but seeing it firsthand was a shock. I'd never seen another supernatural outside of my own family, and that was precisely the way my family had wanted it.

"You're not what I expected a witch to be like," I blurted before I could even stop myself. "I'm sorry, that was very rude of me. I just haven't been around many other people with magic."

Her eyes narrowed into slits.

"I take it manners aren't a part of your résumé? If you absolutely must know, I'm a witch, as are my children and my husband, and every member of our family dating back to the original. So please, be diligent about not using your charms around my children. They are young and impressionable, just beginning to learn about what they are and the roles they will play in this family. I don't want their heads filled with any other rubbish," she snapped, her English accent coming through thickly.

I'd apparently struck a nerve, though it was clear the woman had a great deal of pride in their lineage. It was something I could understand. Marids were a proud race, dating our lines back over a millennium. However, there were a lot of dark spots and blemishes along the way. We could be hard to control. For the most part, we didn't bring up the seedier parts of our history.

Mrs. Grandville circled around me, lips pursed, which made her almost plastic face seem even tighter. I bit my lip, trying to push away the uneasy feeling that churned in my gut. Her heels clicked against the tiled floor, echoing off the stark white walls of the foyer.

"I suppose you'll have to do. This way," she said as she turned and headed through the door and disappeared deeper into the house.

It took me a moment to gather my senses and follow my new employer. The unease hadn't lessened any, and I was beginning to regret my decision to take the job without meeting the family I'd be living with. It was clear she didn't much care for me, but I'd regret not giving this a shot. Experience was experience, even if it was bad.

At the foot of the staircase stood my new charges.

Tabitha and Cornelius, ages eleven and eight.

Luckily, I'd been sent all of the pertinent information about the children, so I wasn't walking in totally blind. The pair stood straight-backed and proper, keeping their stares downcast. Both were startlingly similar in their physical appearance to their mother, right down to the button noses. Tabitha's navy-blue skirt was complemented by a matching sweater vest and a white blouse that made her look older, more akin to a boarding school student in her uniform than an average girl her age. Cornelius was just as proper in his burgundy polo and khaki pants.

"Children, this is your new governess, Ms. Anand. You will make her feel welcome, is that clear?" she asked sternly.

"Yes, ma'am," the pair answered in unison.

"Ms. Anand, these are the children, Tabitha and Cornelius," Mrs. Grandville announced with prideful expectation.

I seized the opportunity, the need to make the best possible first impression my driving force. Placing my bag down, I extended my hand toward Tabitha first and dropped into a crouch so I was eye level with the two.

"Hi, Tabitha. You can just call me Lina if you want to. I won't mind. Same goes for you, Cornelius. I'm new at this, but I think we're going to get along pretty great. What do you think?"

The pair of them eyed my hand like they'd never seen one in their lives before casting wary sideways glances at each other. Mrs. Grandville sighed heavily, making her great disappointment known, frowning deeply.

"You're both dismissed," Mrs. Grandville barked, turning her focus to me. "Ms. Anand, I hope you understand what we're trying to do here. We are raising the next generation of Grandvilles, and such a task requires an immense amount of discipline and structure. The children don't need to be coddled; no one will do that for them in the real world. They need to know what our expectations of them are and prepare themselves accordingly. That's where you come in. You were not hired to be their friend. Have I made myself clear?" she asked icily.

My throat went dry on the spot.

I croaked, "Yes, ma'am."

My brows rose in disbelief. These were children, not soldiers. They needed fun, games, love, friends . . . but who was I to question her rules?

With a curt nod, Mrs. Grandville turned on her heel and climbed up the staircase and into a small hallway beside it. I followed close behind, but we didn't have to travel far. There was only a single door set into the hall's end wall.

"This is your room. All of your belongings are to remain in this room, and guests are not permitted. It is my understanding that you have family who would wish to visit with you, but you'll need to do any visiting in town and ensure that such visits do not interfere with your duties. Understood?" she asked.

I nodded before my mouth outpaced my good sense.

The hope that had begun to take root in my heart turned sour in the span of a moment. I had expected something entirely different than what was being presented to me. I had always enjoyed playing with my young cousins and listening to their wild, imaginative tales, which made me hope I would enjoy working with children. Upon my internet search, I'd found that most nannies became an integral part of the family, one of my many hopes when I'd taken the job. However, Mrs. Grandville was making damn sure I knew I was very clearly an outsider here.

"On the bed, you'll find a list of approved meals, emergency contacts, and schedules. Any outings you wish to take the children on must be first approved by myself or Mr. Grandville. It should also go without saying that as young and impressionable children who are new to their studies, they should not be exposed to certain types of charms," Mrs. Grandville explained.

"So no magic in front of Tabitha or Cornelius?" I clarified.

She nodded.

"All right. That's fine. I'm not really comfortable using it in front of people anyway. You never know who's watching."

"Good. I should also mention that Havenwood Falls is different than other places you may have visited. The supernatural make up a sizeable portion of the population, which, of course, requires a different set of rules. The Court of the Sun and the Moon will need you to be registered in order to stay in the town. Adelaide Beaumont will arrive shortly to begin your tattoo and registration."

"Tattoo?" I questioned.

"Yes, it's fairly simple. There are wards around the town. The tattoos are spelled to work with the wards and serve as your registration. So, get settled as best you can. Ms. Beaumont will arrive shortly."

Without another word, Mrs. Grandville turned and exited the room. As soon as she was clear of the doorway, her hand flicked overhead, and the door swung shut behind her. For someone who was so uptight, she sure flexed her magic when it suited her. The click of her heels echoed as she retreated down the hall and descended the stairs.

I had been dismissed.

Taking in the small room, I tried to remind myself that this experience was what I would make it. The room, albeit small and plain, was a blank canvas; one I could change and shape to suit my needs. And the Grandville children? Well, we'd work on it. There had to be some common ground and wiggle room to be found. That became my new mission, my purpose, and damn it if I was going to let a challenge go unanswered.

Not quite twenty minutes later, there was a knock at my door.

"Come in," I called out, putting the last of my clothes into the drawers I'd been provided.

A girl about my age with light brown hair popped her head inside the door carefully.

"Hi, are you Alina?" she asked, pushing the door open wide enough for her to slip through and shutting it quietly behind her.

"Yeah, you must be Ms. Beaumont," I said, sliding the drawer closed with my hip and extending my hand to her.

She shook my hand firmly as her eyes raked around me and over my body with a warm smile.

"You can just call me Addie. It's very nice to meet you. Has anyone explained what's going to happen or the process?" Addie asked, pulling up a chair and seating herself across from the bed.

"Briefly, but I'm still a bit confused as to why this is necessary."

"I get that all that time. So Havenwood Falls is protected by magical wards," she began, cupping her hand over several bracelets adorning her wrist.

"Yeah, Mrs. Grandville mentioned that part."

"Good. Basically, the wards ensure we don't let just anyone in this town, like those who wish to bring harm. The registry and the tattoos are linked to the wards, so we know who's in town and when someone leaves," Addie explained. "The wards extend to about twenty-five miles beyond the official city limits on all sides, so there's plenty of room to roam. But beyond that, the tattoo disappears and no longer works. As you can imagine, with a town full of supernatural beings, we need to know who's here, why, and how long they plan to stay. You know, so in case something goes bad, we know who to hunt down." She smiled before continuing. "For the most part, everyone gets along without too much trouble, but when they don't, there are consequences, just like with human laws. Number one rule—protect the secret. Do not ever let the humans see you do magic or clue them in to what their neighbors really are."

Finally, the tiny Colorado town was beginning to make sense.

"So that's why there was the in-depth background check before I was offered the position as the Grandvilles' nanny?"

Addie nodded.

"And why the town wasn't on any maps or why I couldn't find any directions to drive myself here?"

"Yep," Addie said, popping the *p* at the end. "So any ideas for a design for your tattoo?"

"Not really. I only just learned of all of this about a half hour ago. The tattoo was a bit of a shock, and I've never had one before."

"Don't worry. I promise it won't hurt. What kinds of things do you think are pretty or catch your eye? What do you like to do? Maybe something to make it easier to access your elemental magic? I'm really flexible. I just need an idea to go on, and I can sketch something out."

"I guess if I had to choose, something feminine in black and grey, maybe on the inside of my forearm? I know that's not very helpful."

"Don't worry about it. Give me a minute to draw something up, and we can go from there. Go ahead and finish unpacking or whatever you still have to do while I'm busy."

"Great," I said weakly.

I didn't handle needles or pain well at all. There wasn't too much that needed to be put away since I'd traveled light. With only having a single bedroom, I didn't have too much space at my disposal, and I hated clutter more than anything.

Addie pulled a pad out of her bag and began to sketch. From where I stood, I couldn't tell what she was drawing, although it looked sort of like some kind of flower. Whatever it was looked intricate . . . likely requiring a whole lot of pokes to finish. Inhaling deeply, I tried not to think about the tattoo or the process and counted to three before exhaling.

"It'll be all right, I promise. I can help you relax if you want me to or even make it so you don't feel a thing." She wiggled her fingers in the air.

I shook my head. "No, thanks. It's not that I wouldn't appreciate it and it's nothing personal, but I just met you. I'm not comfortable with anything more than this right now."

"I totally get it. That's smart by the way, not trusting people too easily. That's how you survive."

"My dad always drilled into my siblings and me the importance of being cautious, especially with our magic," I explained.

"He sounds like a smart man," Addie remarked.

"More like overbearing, but yeah. If it were up to him, I'd never leave home and basically live under a rock where the world doesn't know I exist."

Addie didn't say anything right away, but she stopped what she was doing.

"I can't really blame him there. Don't get me wrong, I see your side of things and I'm the same way, but your kind aren't very common. In fact, I don't believe I've ever met a Marid djinn before. A djinn, yes, but not a Marid."

"How did you know what I was? I haven't really told anyone other than the Grandvilles."

"I have my ways," she said slyly, before flipping the notepad around to show me her completed drawing.

I'd been right when I thought it was a flower, but it was so much more. It was a mandala with eight petals and tiny scrollwork, lines, and dots dancing around its interior. It was stunning and perfect and so very me.

"Do you like it?" Addie asked when I didn't say anything right away.

"Oh yes. It's perfect." My fingers brushed over the delicate design.

Addie pulled her bag onto her lap and withdrew her kit. She unsheathed several needles and began to fill tiny cups with the ink she'd brought with her. I felt like I was watching a surgeon prepare for an open-heart surgery, though nowhere near as dangerous, even if my palms were sweating enough to give that impression.

"Excellent. Let's get started, shall we?" she suggested.

Hesitantly, I sat down across from her. My hands were shaking in spite of my attempts to calm myself.

"Is there a way for you to spell yourself into a calmer state?" she asked.

I nodded. "Yes, but this is something I should suck up and get over. I don't like using my magic as a crutch."

"Oh, well, good for you. Magic can be tempting to abuse. Just let me know if you need to stop, and I'll be happy to."

I squeezed my eyes shut and pushed my arm out toward Addie.

"Let's just do the damn thing," I muttered.

"That's the attitude I like!"

Addie applied the cool stencil to my arm and transferred the image in a bright purple ink. The buzz of the machine filled my ears, making my heart jump in my chest. I turned my face away from Addie and my arm and dug my teeth into my lip. I felt the pressure as Addie touched the needle head to my skin and began tracing the fine lines of the mandala. There was no pain and almost no blood. Shocked at the feather light touch, I turned my face back toward her, watching Addie interestedly.

"Not as bad as you thought it would be?" she asked.

I could hear the smile in her words as she said it.

"Not at all. I'd always heard it hurt, and this is barely more than an annoyance."

"I'm decent at what I do, and these go a little differently than your average tattoo. There's magic in them, so its effect is a little different for everyone, but you're doing great, and your skin looks like it's reacting well to the ink. This should be done in no time at all. Just relax."

And I did.

Addie and I chatted while she worked, learning more about each other. She told me about the town and some of its inhabitants, like being careful about straying onto pack land or into the bears' territory, which I had zero intention of doing anytime soon. She didn't look down on me for what I was or act like she was better than me in any way, not like Mrs. Grandville had. Something told me if given the opportunity, Addie and I could be good friends in time.

I'd been in Havenwood Falls less than two hours, and I'd already found someone whom I could see being friends with. I was going to like my new home, pissy bosses or not.

CHAPTER 4

GABRIEL

*H*ow had I ever forgotten such a place existed? All those memories I'd shared with Viktor had somehow been altered to make me believe they were somewhere else entirely. The witches of Havenwood Falls were clever that way. Their magical wards guarding the town stripped memories from those who left, preventing a massive influx of humans and supernatural beings alike. Things had come back to me like a trickling stream in the spring over the week I'd been in town. Slowly, bits and pieces had been triggered by one thing or another. An image of Viktor and me sitting together, watching the sun rise over the town, came rushing back. That vision was the last time I'd seen the sun's shimmering rays and felt them warm my cool skin. I had to look at the town in an entirely new light.

Despite being absent for forty years, I was surprised to see that Havenwood Falls hadn't changed much. Sure, there were some new businesses and new neighborhoods, but its bones hadn't changed a bit. There was a ski resort—that was a newer addition—but the town still felt the same. I found myself waiting to see Viktor's imposing form walking along the town square, puffing on a cigarette with a beautiful woman on his arm. It was foolish, yet it seemed like he'd never left.

The sun had disappeared below the mountains, casting the town into darkness; however for me, it was time to make my presence known. One of the Luna Coven members would likely be making their rounds to find me. They were the instrument of the Court of the Sun and the Moon to keep track over everyone who wasn't normal or human. The whole setup rubbed me the wrong way. As much as I wanted to tell all those pompous blood bags to suck a dick with their *every supernatural being must check in*, I had to admit being able to feel the warmth of the sun's rays made possible by their damn tattoos was practically a wish come true. As soon as I'd crossed the wards, the Celtic knotted sun had reappeared on my forearm, leaving me rather confused for the next day or so until the memory came back. It was a feat which was impossible anywhere else in the world, but the people in Havenwood Falls had managed to form a mutually beneficial friendship and make such a feat possible.

Mathilde Augustine, accompanied by a much younger woman, approached me, abandoning their oversight of the year's Thanksgiving decorations.

"Gabriel Doyle. I thought that might be you. What brings you back to our town?" the old crone asked.

"Mathilde. It's been a long time. You're looking as sharp as ever," I replied, giving her my most charming smile.

"Elsmed will be wanting to see you straight away," she said, straightening up and looking down her nose at me.

"Elsmed isn't dead yet? Shame," I mused. "I was hoping this town would be rid of that old troll by now."

I harbored no ill will toward anyone in the town, to my knowledge, but that didn't mean that everyone who remembered me was fond of me either. Elsmed was an old goat who, in my honest opinion, would be best avoided whenever possible.

"Still evasive. Some things never change. Are you passing through? Or will you be staying with us a while?"

I hadn't given it much thought, though I was sure the little business I'd have to take care of would take me a few days to sort out.

"Still undecided as to the length of my stay, however I doubt my business should take more than a month, tops."

"Very well, then. *If* you are permitted to stay, it goes without saying that you should behave yourself, what with your past and all. Rumor had it you were a vicious one. I'd be careful if I were you. There are those of us who still remember the stories." Mathilde had a far-off look in her eyes. "It makes me wonder how much a man can really change."

Viktor had told his enemies tales of his bloodthirsty offspring with the hope it would make others think twice before crossing him. It was his own way of showing fatherly pride, and my youth gave way to such tales, but I was centuries apart from that young man. Time had mellowed me, and death had robbed me of my only true companion.

"Well, I hope I can satisfy your curiosity in time. It's been a pleasure as always, Mathilde," I said with a respectful bow of my head, but inside I was seething.

It never failed that when I came to town, I was always met with apprehension and leery stares, my former reputation preceding me.

Without another delay, I made my way through town to the last place I had called home. Viktor's home stood on four acres not far from Havenwood Heights, where the uppity Old Families lived, but so far as I knew, the property had never been sold. Viktor had insisted on creating a trust to keep the home in good repair on the off chance something happened to him. Little did he know he'd have to put that to good use not too long after.

The looming Italianate-styled mansion had been kept up, that much was obvious as I approached it. The front light was on, as was the dining room light to the right of the front door. However, there didn't seem to be anyone there. It was going to be an upgrade from the Whisper Falls Inn, a homecoming of sorts.

I didn't bother knocking and walked right in the front door. That was a good sign. No invitation needed meant no one lived there, or at least no one living. The wooden floors were recently polished, and the scent of fresh paint permeated the air. Lorenzo entered several moments after I did, carrying our bags. He placed them carefully at the foot of the regal staircase, which was the defining feature of the foyer. Despite not making it past the entry parlor, I could already tell it had been kept to my sire's specifications, not a thing about it changed. Not even the paint color, which was an eggshell white.

"Gabriel? Where would you like your bags?" Enzo asked, shaking me from my nostalgia.

"Oh! Right, sorry. It hadn't occurred to me that you haven't been here before. It'll be upstairs to the right. Second door. Feel free to choose any of the other rooms as your own. I don't think I'll have too much need of you during our stay, so consider this a vacation and try not to get into too much trouble."

"Won't you need to feed?"

I shook my head. "I will, but this town has provisions for that. Don't worry about me, old friend. I'll be just fine."

He bowed his head and carried the bags upstairs, disappearing around the corner. Moving to follow him, I heard steps mounting the front porch. Without so much as a knock, the door swung in, and a young woman strode in, eyes wide with shock when they met my own.

"Who are you? What are you doing here?"

I smirked and lifted a brow, leveling her with a knowing stare. The woman had Luna Coven written all over her, every luscious inch. My cock didn't even twitch, though, a sad side effect of my obsessive infatuation. However, that didn't mean I couldn't appreciate a woman's beauty. Surprisingly, she wasn't afraid of me in the least. If she was, she never let on once.

"It's very nice to meet you. My name's Gabriel Doyle, the new owner of this house," I purred.

"Tone it down, Fabio. You're not my type. As for the owner of this house? I was under the impression it had been left in trusts to manage its upkeep. Unless you're Viktor Azimov, which I'd challenge, this house isn't yours, and you're trespassing."

Clever girl, I thought appreciatively.

"You're right. I'm not Viktor, but he was my father, and this was my residence the last time I was here. If it makes no difference to you, I'd just as soon keep to what's familiar to me. This home held many memories, and I've come to pay my respects to Viktor and his legacy.

Which now begs the question, who are you and what are you doing here?"

The girl's eyes narrowed at me like she was weighing what I'd said.

"That wasn't an answer," she noted. "Either way, I'm Addie Beaumont, and I'm here to find out why you're here and keep it all by the book. Elsmed would like to see you right away to ask you some questions. We don't want any trouble here, so I'll need you to follow me. I may be giving you the benefit of the doubt, but if you prove me wrong, you'll regret the day you ever came to this town. Understood?" she announced.

I nodded. "I dare say, it's been a long while since I've been in a woman's company who could command attention the way you do. I appreciate your generosity, and I have no intention of being a nuisance. There's some business I have to attend to and then I suspect I'll be on my way once again. As for the Elsmed business, I get the feeling this isn't a request."

"You'd be correct."

Extending a hand toward the door, I said, "Well, then let's get on with it. I need to work on my tan."

The corner of her lips turned up as though she was trying to suppress a laugh.

"Sure thing, Mr. Doyle," Addie replied, turning on her heel and striding back down the steps, shaking her head as she went.

The meeting with Elsmed had been rather uneventful, a barrage of questions about some Collector, whom I knew nothing about. Though I was surprised the fae agreed to let me stay. He'd always been so open about his disdain and distrust of me. All the same, it was made clear they'd be watching me.

The next morning, I rose earlier than I had in nearly half a century. Wandering through the house, I kept finding myself standing before Viktor's closed bedroom door. Coming to grips with the reality of his loss was one of the goals of my return, and without a sign of my raven-haired beauty, I could think of nothing stopping me from accomplishing that. As I entered Viktor's room, memories flooded my mind, cutting deep, as though the loss was still fresh. I almost didn't notice the envelope sitting on the nightstand beside the bed. Crossing the room, I noted my name scrawled across the back of it in Viktor's elegant hand.

The grandfather clock downstairs chimed loudly, announcing the coming dawn. Stuffing the letter into my pocket, I turned and left the room, sure there was nothing left for me there besides secrets and heartache. Before I even knew what I was doing, I was bounding down the stairs and out the front door.

I wanted to watch the sun rise over the mountains and witness firsthand the sky changing from purple to pink and then orange, just before the sun would rise over the peak and bathe the valley in light. Taking Lorenzo's car, I made my way up Mount Sousa.

By the time I reached the top, the sky had lightened just slightly. There was no better spot to watch the sun rise than right here. I'd found it decades earlier, when the town was smaller than it was now. Finding a clear spot on the rocky ground, I settled in and got as comfortable as possible on hard stone.

As it turned out, being back in town and being given all my memories back had quieted my dreams, much to my dismay. However, being back gave voices to the past, and they'd been growing louder with each moment I stayed.

"Gabriel, one day, I won't be there to tell you what to do or how to live, not that you listen when I do. When that day comes, I want you to know that having you by my side these many years has been a privilege. We may not share blood by birth, but you are my son just the same. Know who you are and where you came from. Don't ever forget it."

Viktor clasped his hand on my shoulder and gave it a hard squeeze before he turned away and left me alone.

I'd been standing in this very place when he'd said those words to me. At the time, I thought his age was making him sentimental, but maybe he knew more than he ever let on. He always seemed to. That was the part most people never saw of him—the raw man who cared for those under his protection. The world saw him as a monster, known for his cruelty and deadly accuracy. In fact, he was all of those things, but there was something underneath all of that which was still more human than beast. That was the Viktor Azimov I'd come to know and love.

Reaching into my pocket, I pulled the envelope out and stared at it. Something told me that whatever its contents, I'd be a changed man after reading it. Sliding my finger under the seal, I pulled the letter out and set to reading.

Gabriel,

I fear my time may be limited, and I know not what tomorrow brings. My hope is that this letter reaches you when the time is right and you can find it in you to take up my reins. The Lilith Nest is dear to me, though I fear there may be a traitor among them. However, the truth is never that simple.

In the event of my demise, it is my most heartfelt wish that you succeed me as the nest leader. I know your mind is troubled and you fear the corruption that power brings, but you have a good head for justice and enough sense to know when to play your cards close to the vest or when to go all in. Be well, Gabriel, and may Lilith ever watch over you.

Viktor.

Re-reading it several more times, I couldn't shake the feeling that my sire had known what was to come. Leading had never interested me, yet Viktor's words wouldn't leave me alone. Would resurrecting the fallen nest be so bad? The Petrans held the Court seat, but they didn't understand the Gothic vampires, not with their pure blood and the knowledge that one day their lives would end—perhaps after many centuries or even millenia, but they'd still end. We faced eternity while everyone we knew and loved faded into distant memories. No, we needed a voice too. Not a Court seat, but something that would unify us and make them take notice. The revelation ignited a fire in my belly that I would no longer be able to ignore. It was time I stepped up to the responsibilities Viktor intended for me.

I stayed a while longer, contemplating what it would take to accomplish such a task. Whatever I did would have to be calculated and careful. The sun rose even higher as the morning wore on. Birds danced among the tree branches, cawing and flitting around like it was choreographed. The town had come to life below. Getting to my feet, I turned and headed back for the car. There was one thing that couldn't wait another day. I needed to pay my respects and finally say farewell to my father's ashes where he'd been laid to rest in the Havenwood Falls Cemetery.

The drive was short enough, although despite having lived in the town for a time, I'd never had need to visit the place before. Standing at the gates of the cemetery, I knew he was in there somewhere. No amount of willing myself to take a step forward would force my feet to cooperate. Pangs of the loss were gnawing at me from somewhere deep in my belly. He'd been my father for far longer than my biological human father ever had. He took a lowly slave and raised me up to a proper gentleman, taught me to survive anything. I still remembered the horror I'd felt when he'd found me on the whipping post, bleeding from the lashes across my back. Tied to the post, there wasn't anything I could do to stop him or defend myself, but that had been for the best.

I'd woken up a few days later in the nearby woods and slaughtered my master and his mistress. Vile scum, the both of them. Viktor had liked what he'd seen in me.

Then, he took me away from the Irish countryside and made me the man I was today. I'd killed my way through all of Europe over the next century or two, long ago when vampires were feared and people were afraid of the night. Times had changed, though, and now people emulated us with their plastic fangs and polyester capes.

My gaze traveled over the iron gate and down to the threshold at my feet. I stepped forward and made my way to the older section of the cemetery.

Seeing his grave marker would make his absence real. Mausoleums stood tall, casting shadows over much of the graveyard. Sunlight filtered down through the bare branches overhead. Chains and cages around tombs, runes and other magical symbols were all necessities, because sometimes the dead didn't like to stay that way. I ducked under the colored glass orbs hanging from branches.

The cemetery was like a maze, reminding me of the times I'd spent in New Orleans—times with Viktor. The Petran vault lay ahead, large and looming, stealing all my attention. I nearly missed the narrow tomb wedged in between two sister Ash trees. In shallow carved letters was Viktor Azimov's name. His birth date as well as his sire date were unknown, but his death date was clear and stark against the granite stone.

I couldn't understand where things had gone so off the rails. Viktor was careful about the people he drank from, almost to the point of being obsessive, but I couldn't deny the facts. I wasn't there for him at the end, and I didn't know the details, nor did I want to.

"Viktor, old friend. How did we get here?" I murmured.

I was met with only silence as I continued.

"Would you still be here if I'd come back to you sooner? I wonder a lot about how different things would be now. If you were here now, I know you'd tell me to quit being a sentimental sap, but I never got the chance to tell you thank you or goodbye. We were supposed to have eternity, though I suppose even an immortal isn't guaranteed tomorrow," I whispered, kneeling in front of the grave.

I dug my fingers into the cold ground at my feet. Earth. One day, we all come back to it and become one. So many things had changed since my time with Viktor Asimov. I'd lost the love of the hunt I'd once had, along with the will to keep going on. Every day was the same as the one before, only the scenery changing. Viktor had been different. He'd understood something I'd never quite figured out—the meaning of life and how to find purpose. He and I had gone our separate ways while I figured out what I wanted to do with the very long life I'd been given, but it wasn't until almost six months ago that I'd finally understood what he'd meant. The dreams that had plagued me were so real, so vivid, that I'd been convinced they were real at first. Then I'd wake and have to face a world where beauty and love were not a part of my life. That was the crux of the reason I'd come back to

Havenwood Falls—something was calling me home and why not give in?

"You know, you once said to me that every dream had a meaning, and sometimes we find what we need the most when we aren't looking for it. I think you're right, you know. I've been having these dreams for months about a woman. She's never told me her name, but by God, I think she's the one, Viktor. She makes me want to live again, more than just existing, more than feeding and traveling. If you can hear me, old friend, please give me a sign. Show me what I'm supposed to do now."

I wasn't sure what I expected would happen. Perhaps I hoped he'd step out of the shadows and impart one of his gems of wisdom, but I was met with only the tinkling of wind chimes and the breeze cutting through the thin branches overhead. Thick clouds were rolling in.

"Viktor, I'm sorry I wasn't there at the end. You deserved better than the way it all ended, but I came here for a reason. That letter you left me—I got the message loud and clear. Your legacy will live on, I promise. I came to say goodbye, and I hope you have found peace at last. *Solas Mhic Dé ar a anam*," I said, letting the old Irish Gaelic roll off my tongue with ease.

Turning away from the grave, I made my way back toward the car, leaving Viktor in the past where he belonged. The future was going to be what I made it, and I wanted to start by settling some old business. My time up on the mountain had given me clarity. Viktor's nest had been decimated by the massacre, and it was high time someone stepped up and took it back. My first stop was going to be downtown —convincing the right people was going to take some strategy.

I climbed into the black Lexus and took off, checking off the names of the founding families I'd need to convince. I pulled into an open spot along Eleventh Street and climbed out, heading toward the south side of the town square. Rounding the corner, I pulled my sleeve back into place, effectively covering the sun tattoo on my arm. My eyes were adjusting slowly to the sunlight, forcing me to squint so I didn't run into anyone. The wind suddenly kicked up and shifted directions, forcing me to stop dead in my tracks.

There was a scent that had taunted me for months in my dreams. Had I fallen asleep? Was it all a dream?

I scanned the street, searching for my raven-haired goddess as I entered Town Square Park.

Then I saw her.

She was busy finding a seat at a table. Glancing at the sign, I realized it was a café. Comfortable and public, it wasn't my first choice for meeting her the first time in person, but who was I to look a gift horse in the mouth? There was a large part of me that was waiting for her lush form to evaporate before my very eyes, teasing me with what I wanted most, but never thought I could have.

Her face turned toward me, and I would've sworn that if my heart was beating, it would've been pounding its way out of my chest. It was undoubtedly her.

The woman's gaze locked with my own, and for a brief moment, the world stopped and fell away, leaving only the two of us. A smile stretched my face for the first time I could recall in what seemed like years. Our moment was over too soon as something caught her attention, and she tore her stare away from my own.

My head was spinning, and I needed a moment to regain my composure. Moving quickly, I ducked into the town square and headed for the gazebo. What the hell had just happened? Replaying everything, it dawned on me that when we had locked eyes, there was a flash of recognition. She recognized me just as I had her.

A hard knot formed in the pit of my belly. Was the woman of my dreams just a figment of my imagination? I needed to know she was real if there was ever a hope of making our dreams a reality.

CHAPTER 5

ALINA

The week was going absolutely horribly. In fact, I wasn't sure the Grandvilles would keep me on much longer—if I wanted to stay on, and that was questionable. The family was difficult, but having checked my bank account, I couldn't easily walk away from that kind of money. It put me in a difficult spot.

Mrs. Grandville didn't seem to be satisfied with a damn thing I did. Every single day there was a barrage of new complaints. Tabitha and Cornelius were miserable, and I could see why. Their mother was an impossible woman, and their father was practically absent from their lives. He'd show up for dinner and eat silently before disappearing—whether to an office or somewhere else, I didn't know. I wasn't sure what he did for a living or in any other aspect of his life, and I hadn't worked up the courage to ask or speak more than a cordial greeting.

The children were too quiet, like they were afraid to interact with anyone other than each other. Being homeschooled as they were, I could understand how they'd become so withdrawn. It made me wonder what they'd been subjected to before I'd arrived. I hadn't been able to find a way to connect with them, yet. They never said much more than "yes, ma'am" or "no, ma'am." Sometimes I thought I could detect the glimmer of a protest in Cornelius—whom I'd taken to calling Neil—but he never voiced it. The day was coming when he'd rebel, and that day was going to be spectacular.

When I'd taken on the position, I'd done so with the thought that I would have some time to myself. That wasn't the case. It was all-consuming. The Grandvilles quite simply didn't have time for or interest in their children, leaving the entirety of their care to me. It was Saturday, and technically my day off, if I were to go by my contract, yet I was still scared of upsetting my employer if she had other plans for me. I'd given quitting some thought, knowing that sometimes jobs just didn't work out. However, going back to Denver wasn't an option, not when I knew my dad would hold it over my head with I-told-you-so's until I was old and gray. My thoughts returned to my current situation.

Frustration and worry were quickly becoming a constant in my life. I needed a break. Not a vacation or anything, but a couple hours to unwind among people who didn't make me feel like I was balancing on a knife's edge.

With a newly found steely resolve, I decided I was going in to town. I wanted to explore my new home and find two things. The first was where to get an excellent cup of coffee, and the second was more or less anything that would encourage something resembling a social life. The house was quiet; it was still early.

As I crept down the stairs, I stopped near the bottom when I noticed I didn't hear any noise coming from the residents. The door was in view from where I stood frozen. The familiar clinking of Mrs. Grandville's heels echoed in the hall upstairs. There was a sense of urgency in those steps, and I couldn't risk angering her further.

I bolted for the door, slipping out in near silence. Even the door was helpful as it shut silently and the hinges didn't creak or groan when jostled. Keeping my pace brisk, I turned onto the sidewalk and followed the streets toward the center of town. It was relaxed compared to the bustle of the weekends I was accustomed to in Denver, but surprisingly, I liked it. The whole town felt quaint and picturesque. If I hadn't needed to register when I'd arrived, I never would have guessed that so many different supernatural beings resided here. It made me look at every single person I passed or spied doing yard work a little differently.

The town was different than any I'd ever seen, like a floating island in the sky, unreachable from the outside. That was exactly how it felt as I gazed at the mountains surrounding the oasis. The scent of freshly roasted coffee and buttery pastries invaded my nostrils, drawing me closer to the shop. The sign for Coffee Haven was straight ahead of me.

Stop numero uno, I thought.

Something so tantalizing had to be made with magic. I'd never smelled something so wonderful in my life, and I was by no means unfamiliar with coffee shops or bakeries. Pushing open the door, I was met with the chiming of the welcome bell. There was already a short line, but it seemed to be moving quickly, so I staked my place in line and carefully contemplated the menu.

When it was my turn, I stepped up to the counter and smiled warmly at the barista who was waiting patiently with an intrigued stare. My eyes dipped to the name tag on her shirt: *Harlow*. She looked to be about the same age I was and was watching me with an amused grin.

"You're new in town, aren't you?" she asked without coming off as accusing.

"What gave me away?" I chuckled, the tips of my ears heating when I thought of being so clearly out of place.

"Small town. You get to know everyone real quick. And most people have their favorites memorized and don't usually give it much thought, unless you're a tourist, and you don't really strike me as the type," she noted, one side of her mouth lifting in a half smile.

"Nope, not a tourist, but I'll take any caffeinated drink you'd recommend and same with a pastry."

"No allergies?" she asked.

I shook my head.

"All right. Go ahead and grab a seat. I'll bring it out in just a moment."

"What do I owe you?" I asked, surprised she hadn't given me the total yet.

"Don't worry about it. This one's on me. Welcome to Havenwood Falls."

I nodded my thanks, headed to an open table near the window to put my things down, and returned to the counter, finding a sunny spot while I waited. Standing near the front window, I glanced around the café, watching the patrons as they sipped their drinks and munched on their snacks. The sensation of being watched sent shivers up my spine and gooseflesh over my body. No one in the coffee shop was paying me any attention. I cast a quick glance out the window, and that's when I saw him.

Across the street and several yards to the right stood a man in the doorway of the park's gazebo. He was tall and well dressed, like a businessman. At first, I thought maybe he was checking out the café, but that wasn't right either, because his stare was fixed on me. His build and face reminded me of the man from my dreams, but that wasn't possible. He wasn't real, though the resemblance was uncanny.

My nipples pebbled, pushing against the restraints of my bra and T-shirt as warmth flooded my core. It was the most visceral reaction I'd ever had to a man before.

I bit my lip, giving the man a coy smile. I didn't know him from Adam, and I couldn't be too careful. There was something in his stare that held me, and I couldn't tear my gaze away from him no matter how much I wanted to. He didn't move, frozen in the moment just as I was. Even though he was easily fifty feet away, I could practically feel the warmth of his breath on my skin as though he was right next to me. The blue of his eyes was bright like glacier ice, and the corner of his mouth ticked up in a smirk.

"Here we go. One café americano and a blueberry scone. Cream and sugar are over there next to the counter if you need any. Can I get you anything else?" the barista asked cheerily, breaking whatever hold the mystery man had over me.

I turned away from him, stunned into silence. I blinked a few times quickly before I could muster a response.

"No, actually. That should be it. Thank you so much."

The girl nodded and turned, disappearing behind the counter. My eyes darted back to where the man had been standing, but he was gone. I turned toward the window, searching for any sign of him along the street, but there was nothing.

Had I imagined the whole thing? Was he not really there? To be honest, I wasn't really sure. Though no one could ever be sure of anything in a town full of what should be impossible. If he was real, and that was a decidedly big *if,* then there was no doubt in my mind he was much more than human. Whatever he was, I doubted he was a djinn like me. A warlock maybe or even a shifter, if his stubbly face was a distinguishing sign.

Making my way to my table, I settled in and picked up the cup of steamy coffee, bringing it to my lips and inhaling the rich aroma. It was really strong and slightly bitter. Cream and sugar wouldn't have been a bad idea. Glancing around the room, I realized no one was paying attention to me. Getting up and leaving my purse behind, I moved to the counter, pouring a teaspoon of sugar and enough cream to fill the cup to the brim.

When I turned back, my table was no longer vacant. I froze, nearly spilling my coffee with the abrupt stop. In the seat across from my own sat the mystery man. His back was to me, but I could tell it was him. Same dark clothes, same wide shoulders and straight posture.

He is real! I thought, trying to calm my breathing and slow my pounding heart. Straightening myself out, I squared my shoulders and strode for the table as though nothing was amiss. I sat in my seat and placed the coffee on its saucer before giving the man a once-over.

His eyes were just as blue as I'd thought they were, maybe even more so, and his lashes were so long I was jealous. His nose was straight and regal, while his lips were full and luscious. I couldn't help but wonder what he tasted like. Dark hair crowned his head with one of those sexy-man haircuts, longer on top and short on the sides.

"I'm Gabriel Doyle. Have we met before?" he asked, extending his hand across the table.

I placed my hand in his. "Alina Anand. Those eyes—you remind me of someone," I said, blurting out exactly what I was thinking.

I wanted to hide as soon as my words made their way to my ears. *Could I have been any cheesier? Way to go, Alina. This is why you don't have boyfriends. Open mouth, insert foot.*

Gabriel's hand was cool to the touch as his long, slender fingers wrapped around my hand. There was a very distinct restrained power in his light touch. It was an exhilarating mix. His thumb ran over the back of my hand, sending chills shooting through the rest of my body like an electric shock.

Something about the man emboldened me, and I realized that had to be a part of the thrill. I didn't know him, and he knew nothing about me. I could be anyone I wanted to be.

"Are you new to town?" he asked, leaning forward so no one near could overhear our conversation.

I nodded.

"I used to live here myself, but admittedly, it's been a very long time since I've been home," Gabriel said, his voice smooth like rich caramel.

"How long is a long time?" I asked, noting the way he'd emphasized the *long*.

The man wasn't human; his presence was just so *extra* it didn't seem possible. That and his good looks were practically Hollywood-ready, intensified by a deadly edge.

Gabriel's eyes narrowed slightly, and the corner of his mouth ticked up in amusement. An image of the same smirk flashed through my thoughts at the same time his smile widened to show his dimples in his cheeks.

"You're an observant one, aren't you?" he noted, glancing around the café before his eyes returned to me, and he withdrew his touch. "Let's just say, my . . . family's . . . roots go back to the mid-seventeenth century."

My mouth popped open. Mid-seventeenth century? That would make him over three hundred fifty years old! I had so many questions, and it only fueled my desire to know what this man was.

I opened my mouth to say more, but Gabriel's hand brushed mine, making me pause. All my focus was on the small stretch of flesh where our bodies touched. Maybe it was the tingling of my magic under my skin in the excitement or maybe it was his. Either way, we had a chemistry that couldn't be denied, and then there was the confounding thoughts that he was too familiar to me to have never met him before.

"Why don't we get out of here and go somewhere quieter and less populated?" he suggested, eyeing the rest of the café's patrons and keeping his voice at a barely audible whisper.

I was playing with fire, and I knew it. Gabriel was a total stranger to me and could kill me without too much of an effort. Granted, I wasn't without my own charms and abilities, but I didn't think I could kill an immortal.

"Do you have any plans to kill me?" I asked, not expecting a straight answer, but braving it all the same.

Gabriel's lips pursed at my question before turning down in a frown.

"No. Although I'd be lying if I said you didn't smell wonderful or that I don't want just a taste, but I have a great deal of self-control, and one thing I can promise is you'll never have cause to fear me . . . as long as you don't try to kill me first. Then all bets are off," he said with a wink.

Vampire.

I didn't know how I hadn't seen it before. The cool skin, longevity, and his air of lethality—they were practically dead giveaways. Yet, instead of being afraid, it was exhilarating sitting across from a being so powerful I couldn't help but to be on edge.

I spied the barista in my periphery. She was watching us with interest, but her face betrayed nothing of her thoughts.

"All right. I'll do it," I answered before I could take it back.

His face morphed into a beaming smile, as though he'd just closed the biggest deal of his life, and maybe he had. Something was telling me everything I knew was about to change. What more could I do than welcome it?

Gabriel signaled for the barista's attention and got a to-go cup for my coffee and a bag for my pastry. Tracking his every movement, I couldn't help admiring the grace with which he moved. Being clumsy on my best days, it made me especially envious. Gabriel returned with everything packed up and ready to go.

"If you want to bail, now is your chance," he joked, extending his hand toward me.

Maybe it was the devil on my shoulder, or maybe just the inner me begging for adventure, but I didn't even think twice before I placed my hand in his. His slender fingers wrapped around mine firmly. As soon as his cool skin met mine, I saw a flash of the two of us on a balcony and in a bed, his lips ravaging the tender flesh just under my ear. My core heated at the image, igniting a long-buried desire that would no longer be ignored.

I blinked and was back in the café, bedrooms and sensual caresses vanished and leaving me almost panting. My face heated, and my ears felt like they were on fire with the embarrassment of being caught.

"Such a beautiful shade of pink," Gabriel remarked, lifting his hand and running an appraising finger down my cheek, following my jaw line to my chin. "On an even more beautiful woman."

Good Lord! Doesn't he know flattery will get him anything his heart desires? I thought heatedly.

"Anything? Is that so?" he teased.

"Any—" I began, then stopped as realization dawned. "Wait a second!"

Gabriel didn't utter a single word, only giving me a quick wink before extending his arm for me to take and escorting me out of the café. The man was full of surprises and could read minds, so it would seem.

We strolled at a leisurely, much slower pace than I wanted. I had too many questions, and the streets were far too crowded to ask such things without taking the risk of being overheard. Gabriel pulled me along toward a small park right across from the library.

After we'd walked for several minutes, the street cleared out a bit, and no one was close enough to overhear what I wanted to know.

"Yes, I can read minds, though I make a point to try not to.

Invading your privacy is not my goal, but your particular line of thinking caught my attention, and you were practically projecting it at me. If it bothers you, all you need to do is say so, and I will endeavor to shut that down when I am around you."

I sighed. "I shouldn't be surprised, given what I've heard of this town already, but I was under the impression vampires didn't have those kinds of abilities."

"Ah, yes. But there's no other place like it. As for the mind reading itself, my kind doesn't have those extra capabilities . . . usually. I made the rather unfortunate mistake of killing the daughter of a voodoo priestess in my younger and more reckless days. She cursed me to never have a moment's silence in the hopes I'd go mad and be put down. It backfired, and while it can be annoying at times, it has its uses. I gather you don't have much experience with other species?" he asked, taking a seat on a shaded park bench near the entrance.

"No. My family likes to stay closer to our own kind."

"And what kind might that be? A siren, perhaps?" he asked, following my stare to the three-tiered bronze fountain, the crowning jewel of Cook's Corner Park. The bronze mermaid statue shone brightly in the November sunlight.

"I . . . really shouldn't. It's nothing personal, but I just met you. If anyone knows what I am, it could put me in a dangerous situation, and there are too many other people who could be put in harm's way."

"You play your cards close to the vest. I can appreciate that, and don't worry, I have nothing to gain by deceiving you or abusing your trust. In fact, I'd much prefer the opposite," Gabriel explained carefully.

I wasn't one of the lucky species who could detect lies just by hearing someone's voice. Even as a stranger, Gabriel was being bluntly honest with me, and that wasn't something I was accustomed to. In my personal experience, most people rarely told the truth even in simple, mundane situations. However, Gabriel's words rang true to me. I believed him, even if he was a vampire and the whole outrageous situation went against my better judgment.

"Do you believe in fate, Alina?" Gabriel asked, getting to his feet and plucking a dying brown leaf from a low-hanging branch overhead.

His contemplative tone shook me from my own wandering thoughts.

"I do. Three days before the Grandvilles contacted me, my father had begun putting pressure on me to find a husband and settle down. That's what women in my family do; they settle. He'd pick a man for me and expect me to go through with the whole ridiculous farce without complaint. I'd be among my own kind and safe. It would've been a great plan, if not for it being the furthest thing from what I wanted. Fate brought me that job to save me from a miserable life, and I ended up here, with you," I mused, smirking at him.

I didn't mention what I wanted to. He likely wouldn't take well my dreaming about him for months on end before ever meeting him.

"How can you be sure?" Gabriel asked, listening carefully to every word.

"Because for the first time in my life, I feel like I'm exactly where I'm supposed to be," I said, giving Gabriel's hand a sure squeeze.

He nodded like he understood. "Wise beyond your years, it would seem."

Gabriel's mouth turned down in a frown, and he leveled me with an uncertain stare before glancing away and inhaling deeply.

"There's something I must ask you, and I would like it if you could hear me out before writing this off as insane, okay?" he asked, his brows knitting together and forming a deep worry line between them.

I nodded.

"I am a dream walker, though I didn't discover this until recently . . . because of you."

"Me?" I squeaked, eyes widening at the accusation. "Why me?"

He smiled, taking my hand between his strong ones. Gabriel's thumb traced the faint blue lines of my veins on the back of my hand.

"I don't rightly know why, but—"

I sat up a little straighter, frowning in an odd mix of confusion and curiosity.

"It was all real," I murmured.

"The dreams?" he questioned.

I nodded, gulping and trying to wet my now parched mouth.

"Yes, they were as real as you and me sitting here. Though, I must confess, it's because of those dreams that I stand before you now. I've searched for you for months, hoping beyond hope that you were real, and not just a figment of a desperate imagination, but here you are. Just like you said you'd be.

"I said? I have no recollection of that, but I can't say I'm sorry for it," I said quickly, surprised at my candidness.

He lifted his hand to my cheek, his deft fingers tracing the planes from just below my ear to my chin.

"I could never be sorry for it. Thank you for giving me hope again," Gabriel admitted.

The butterflies in my belly turned into falcons, battering my insides with their tickling wings.

"I believe you. If it weren't for all these images of the two of us together, I might not, but there's no denying it now. So many nights I spent wishing for sleep just so I could dream. Now I know it was all real, well . . . mostly."

It was true. I couldn't ignore our shared history.

"We've shared more nights than I can recall and seen a dozen cities across the world. We've explored every inch of each other . . . for months. You never gave me your name, but I could never forget those big brown eyes. You, my desert rose, are what brought me back home to Havenwood Falls."

Desert rose.

Pet names had never been my cup of tea, but with Gabriel it fit. My day off was quickly becoming the strangest day I'd had in a while, in the best way possible.

I opened my mouth to say something, but I was cut off by the shrill ring of the phone buried in my purse.

"Shit! Sorry, one second," I rushed out, opening my purse and rifling through its contents to find the device.

The third ring blared loudly by the time I fished it out and caught a glimpse of the caller.

Mrs. Grandville.

"I'm so sorry. I've got to take this," I explained as I rose and strode several paces away. "Hello?"

Without so much as a greeting, Mrs. Grandville's mom-voice filled my ear. "Where are you?"

"Umm, the park?" I quipped, treading carefully.

"The park. That's just great. Where are you supposed to be?"

I didn't have an answer. It was expressly written in my terms of employment that Saturdays and Sundays were my days off.

"Getting Tabitha and Cornelius ready for piano lessons, that's where!"

"Mrs. Grandville, I think there's been a miscommunication or a misunderstanding—" I said, but before I could finish, the line went dead.

She'd hung up on me. *Fuck!*

I turned to see Gabriel watching me intently. His brows were drawn down in concern, and there was a spark of irritation in his stare.

"That was my boss. I-I have to go. I'm so sorry, but I would like to see you again, if I haven't already blown my chance."

His chin dipped once. "I understand."

I didn't know what more to say. Gabriel's words were still playing over and over in my head, and I didn't know what to make of them. Meeting him had been by chance, however seeing him again was going to be very deliberate. Taking a chance, I took a step toward him and then another, until we were only separated by a few inches.

"Gabriel? I don't know you, but I want to. Will I see you again?"

"Of course, love. It takes a lot more than a bitchy boss to scare me off. Tomorrow, by the skating rink. Two o'clock."

I frowned. "I'll probably have Tabitha and Neil with me tomorrow."

"The more, the merrier." His smile was warm and genuine.

Was this real life? Did men like him really exist? I was beginning to hope.

"Alrighty then, tomorrow at two by the skating rink it is. I'll see you then," I said, tucking my hair behind my ears.

I pulled my lip between my teeth and bit down slightly as I smiled. Biting my lip was a nervous habit I'd had since I was at least four years old. No one had been able to break me of it.

Gabriel took my hand in his and brought it to his mouth. He pressed a sensual kiss against my knuckles that threatened to make my knees buckle under me. It was my luck that he noticed the reaction and smirked, showing off his panty-melting dimples in each cheek.

Good Lord, this man is going to be the end of me!

"Until tomorrow," he whispered with a wink, before turning on his heel and striding away from me and out of the park entirely.

I'm not saying I watched him leave, at least not the whole time, but the man had a butt that could make a fine cowboy in a pair of Wranglers look like a chump. When he disappeared from view, I made my way home.

The walk back was over quicker than I was ready for. Thoughts and questions ran rampant through my mind, only begging more questions. I couldn't fathom what Mrs. Grandville had meant about needing to be there for the kids on my designated day off. Surely, she had just gotten confused about which day it was. That had to be it. Throughout the walk back, I alternated between a speed walk and a slow mosey. Mrs. Grandville seemed like the sort of woman who'd be a force to be reckoned with, and I had no interest in crossing her, but I also wasn't going to allow myself to be her doormat, at her beck and call. I had a life too, and I needed her to respect that if our arrangement was ever going to work.

I groaned as the house came into view. *Well, here goes nothing.* I marched myself right up to the house and tried to enter as quietly as I could, but as soon as I stepped through the door, Mrs. Grandville was on me.

"Where were you?" she demanded.

"Oh, um, I wanted to check out the town."

Mrs. Grandville scoffed. "I needed you here. Tabitha and Cornelius have piano lessons in an hour. What was I supposed to do if you weren't here?"

Mrs. Grandville's anger was palpable. Her words and indignant consternation were starting to piss me off. As someone who claimed to be a stickler for the contract, she sure missed the part that stated what days I had off and for myself.

Mrs. Grandville turned to leave and made it a full two steps before my mouth had a full disconnect from my brain and got squirrely.

"Um, take them yourself?" I mumbled, low enough that I was sure no one could hear me.

She froze, turning her face slightly toward me, but said nothing before continuing her exit from the room. I wanted to demand why I was still responsible for the children on the days off she had appointed herself. But I wasn't that brave. I'd have to bring it up later, when she'd had time to calm down and hopefully forget anything she may or may not have heard.

Fuck my life, that was way too close. I needed to get a damn grip on my mouth before I backtalked my way right to the unemployment line and my parents' front door. Which reminded me, I had yet to make a few calls. Pulling the phone out of my back pocket, I quickly typed out a message to my mom that I missed everyone and would call soon. I hadn't called home yet, and still wasn't sure I was ready to.

CHAPTER 6

GABRIEL

Sitting across from the woman who had taunted me in my dreams, always staying just out of reach and without an identity, had been the true test of my resolve. It had taken everything in me not to steal her away and make her mine in every way that counted.

When I saw her—*Alina*—in the window of the coffeehouse, I almost couldn't believe it. For the first time in well over a hundred years, I felt alive again. Excitement flowed through me, where before her there was nothing. I couldn't begin to explain the depths of my feelings, and I didn't know what they meant yet. How many nights had I forced sleep just for the hope of seeing her again? How many times had I told her my darkest secrets without ever seeing her shrink away from my touch when she discovered the monster I was? No. She never needed protection from me, and if the woman turned out to be much different than the fantasy, then so be it. I'd live the rest of my life waiting for the dreams. For the time being, though, I wanted to know everything I could about Alina Anand.

When her phone had rung, it had taken all of my resolve to not steal her away for myself. I was selfish like that, and I didn't care. Her job be damned. Instead, I'd held my tongue and watched as she walked away, back to her employer. I'd followed her home, keeping my distance. There weren't any nefarious intentions behind it, merely wanting to know where she was staying. I'd overheard the way Mrs. Grandville had spoken to her, and I didn't like it. She was too controlling. Alina had been thinking rather loudly, giving me no other option than to listen to what she had to convey. I heard everything the woman had said to her since she'd been hired. Talk about a control freak.

"Gabriel?" Enzo nudged me, shaking me out of my own head.

"Hmm?"

"We're here," Enzo answered, pointing to the lettering on the building.

Bishop Enterprises, Inc.

The Bishops were a difficult bunch, to say the least. Roman Bishop was among the worst. Never doing anything without personal gain, he was exactly the sort I needed to convince. If the Lilith Nest Viktor left behind was to be resurrected, I needed as many aces up my sleeve as I could manage.

"You picked up the Cadenhead?" I asked.

Lorenzo nodded from the driver's seat, handing the bag over his shoulder.

"Excellent," I said, pushing the door open and climbing out of the back seat.

Straightening myself, I strode into the building like I owned the place. The bag was hefty in my hand. I'd remembered Roman's penchant for good whiskey, a topic I was well versed in. There was a secretary typing hurriedly on her tablet, oblivious to me.

I cleared my throat, raising a brow.

"Can I help you, sir?" she asked, not looking up from her screen.

"I'm here to see Roman Bishop. I have an appointment. The name's Gabriel Doyle."

The secretary clicked away on her computer like she hadn't heard a word I'd said. After another moment, she replied, "All right, Mr. Doyle. You can take a seat. He'll be right with you."

I nodded and walked to the sitting area where black leather sofas and chairs sat invitingly.

"No need to sit, Doyle," a deep voice said from the doorway. "Yours is a face I didn't think I'd be seeing again. What dragged you back into town?" he asked, as we passed through the door and entered his office.

Roman Bishop didn't look like he'd aged a day in the last forty years. His dark hair was slicked back, and his jaw was covered by the scruff of a few-days'-old beard. Deep blue eyes observed my every move, calculating, just as I was sizing him up. He was an imposing man, standing a few inches taller than my own six foot one frame. He was lean, but lethal.

"I brought a gift," I said, holding the bag out to him. "You preferred high quality whiskey the last I knew. I figured those tastes didn't change much. Once a whiskey man, always one."

"Cadenhead 1963, excellent cask. Impressive," he noted, examining the bottle for authenticity.

"Whiskey was one thing we Irish got right," I answered.

"No shit. So what is it I can do for you, Doyle? I don't have many visitors bringing gifts or stopping by just for shits and giggles. You came here because you want me to do something for you. What is it?"

Shrewd and to the point. I could respect that.

"Indeed. Viktor Azimov's nest, actually."

"What about it?"

"I want it resurrected. My kind need to stick together, for both our sake and the general public's. By resurrecting the nest, we'd accomplish both."

"What's wrong with the way things are now?"

"You want more power in this town. You're going to need support to get it. What better support than the vampires? You reap the benefits no matter what happens."

"How's that?"

"The vampires support you. In turn, you also get another level of security to keep the vampire population under wraps. Nest members would have to answer to the nest leader in addition to the Petran girl. We keep to ourselves, less problems for you, more autonomy for us. It's a win-win."

"You assume a lot about me."

"When you live as long as I do, you observe, watch choices over time. If I were you, I'd be less worried about me noticing your business dealings and a little more concerned about the other founders noticing," I replied, getting to my feet. "Think it over and give me a call."

I held my hand out to him, waiting for him to shake it. After a moment of contemplation, he thrust his hand into mine, squeezing it in a show of dominance.

"Thank you for the whiskey," he said.

I nodded and strode from the room. Dealing with supes was like a game of chess. The moment you blinked, your adversary could take advantage and win the game. That was precisely what I intended to do.

Checkmate, motherfucker.

When I'd first come back to town, I hadn't known why I was being pulled back. At first, I thought it was Alina, and a part of me still thought it was, but now that I was here, it had to be more than just her. Enzo had done some digging for me while I'd been finishing up some business and spending time with Alina. There hadn't been another well-organized nest since the Lilith Nest had been wiped out in 2005. The massacre had left most too scared to even think of such a thing. The town had sunk its hooks into me, and I was laying down roots. With the nest established and Alina by my side, I wouldn't need anything more.

Neither were mine yet, but things were happening, and I had a plan. I only needed to wait until she fell asleep, and then she would know exactly why she was destined to be mine.

CHAPTER 7

ALINA

The sun was in the final leg of its descent by the time we returned home from their piano lessons. Mrs. Grandville was nowhere to be found, but there was an empty wine glass sporting her signature mauve lipstick next to the sink.

As more evidence of their self-reliance, within thirty minutes of us arriving home, the kids had showered and gotten into pajamas before settling in to read their nightly books.

With the kids tucked in for the night, my time was now officially my own. I ventured upstairs and slunk into my room. Instantly, I could tell something was off. Things were almost where I'd left them, yet not quite. The drawer of the nightstand was slightly ajar, and my jewelry box next to the lamp sat sideways. The more I surveyed the room, the more I noticed was off. Nothing was missing, though.

Someone had rifled through my belongings, and yet, they hadn't taken a single item. Tabby and Neil had been with me, so it couldn't have been either of them, leaving their parents as the prime suspects. This sort of shit was way not cool, and there was no way I was going to put up with my privacy being invaded and not having my boundaries respected. With Mrs. Grandville nowhere to be found, I'd have to brave it and deal with Mr. Grandville.

The house was quiet as I poked my head out of my room.

Mr. Grandville was in his study, hunched over an old dusty book with a tumbler of scotch in his other hand. His face had a red flush to it that said he'd been drinking for a while. Second thoughts crept in. Drunk people were unpredictable, and this was one I didn't even know a little bit about. Remembering the disheveled bedroom, I raised my hand and knocked on the door with as much confidence as I could muster.

The man within grumbled something unintelligible before I could hear him approaching the door. I took a step back to give both of us some room before I was met with the surprised face of Alistair Grandville.

"Ms. Anand? Can I help you with something?" he asked, being more cordial than his wife had ever been.

"Actually yes. There was something I wanted to discuss with you, if you have a moment," I replied, twisting my hands together behind my back in a futile attempt to remain calm.

Confrontation was just about my biggest fear.

"Sure, come right in. I'm actually glad you stopped by. There was something I wanted to speak with you about, too," Mr. Grandville countered, holding the door open wide.

He didn't move out of the doorway, though, so I had to squeeze by him awkwardly. He smelled of a cheap cologne and heavily of his scotch. He had to have been drinking for a while, but you couldn't tell by his movements or speech. His office was about the same size as my room, with bookshelves covering two walls. Most of the titles weren't in English and looked like they'd be better locked away behind a glass case, with how aged they appeared to be. In the corner sat a small bar cart that looked well used.

"What did you wish to speak to me about?" he asked, rounding the edge of his desk and flopping down into his seat.

I took the seat across the desk and answered immediately in the most confident voice I could muster.

"Well, it appears that someone has been in my room and going through my things. While I have nothing to hide, I also won't tolerate my privacy being invaded like that. I need certain assurances that it won't happen again if I'm to continue on here. Otherwise, I'm afraid I'll need to resign."

Mr. Grandville's eyebrows rose, and his lips curled into a smile.

"Self-assured. I like that. It takes balls to stick up for yourself. As for your room, that was my fault. You see, the room used to be my den. Some of the furniture, like the small desk and the bedside table, stayed there. I was looking for a very specific object, and I had worried I may have left it in the desk. I searched for it, but alas, it wasn't there. I do apologize, and I realize I should have asked first, but I'm sure you can understand that I wouldn't be used to asking permission to look for something in my own home. It won't happen again, but this has been an adjustment for all of us. I hope it won't be a factor if you decide you have to leave us," Mr. Grandville explained remorsefully.

I nodded.

"As long as I have your guarantee that it won't happen again, I don't see why it should be an issue. I enjoy your children and would hate to leave, but I can only handle so much," I added.

Mr. Grandville stood and came around the desk until he was right beside me. He sat back against the edge of the desk and crossed his arms over his chest. His blond hair had been gelled back at some point, but it was wearing off and falling loose onto his forehead. His cheeks were flushed with intoxication, getting worse by the minute, but he didn't even act affected.

When he didn't say anything, I figured it was a great time to ask what he'd wanted to speak to me about.

"You mentioned you wanted to speak to me about something as well?" I prodded.

"Right! Erm, I apologize. How rude of me. Can I offer you a drink?" he asked, pushing himself off the desk and taking a few sure strides to where the cart stood.

My mother's voice echoed in the back of my mind: *Never accept a drink from strangers.*

"No, thank you. I'm not much of a drinker."

Nor had I been since I'd gotten drunk the first time and had promptly thrown up all over Bobby Stevens, my first real boyfriend, when I was eighteen.

Mr. Grandville nodded and refilled his own glass before resuming his spot inches away from me, perched on the edge of the desk. After a few moments of awkward silence aside from the ice tinking the side of his glass, he finally got to his point.

"So, you're a Marid djinn, is that right?" he asked.

Normally it wasn't something I went around advertising. Granting wishes came with too many strings attached, and I tried to steer clear of that at all costs. My magic was my own, and it needed to stay that way. However, there wasn't so much as an ounce of malevolence coming from the man, only genuine curiosity.

"I am," I answered.

His smile grew wider, and he leaned in closer.

"That's fascinating! I've read about your kind before, though I never thought I'd have the opportunity to meet one. I have so many questions I could ask you. I'm not sure if you're aware or not, but the history of the djinn race is amazing. Truly extraordinary that any of you survived."

The djinn weren't a species many knew much about, and that was the way we liked it. If he had a lot of information about my kind, I had to wonder why.

"What is it you do for a living, Mr. Grandville?"

"Please. Call me Alistair," he said, his English accent light, but still there. "I specialize in antiques, as those in my family had before me. It's really more of a family business."

"I'm sorry, *Alistair*. I don't know much about antiques. History was never my forte," I replied, slightly confused by what was going on.

Something didn't seem right, yet I couldn't put my finger on what.

"Would you be able to give me a small demonstration? Just to sate the curiosity of another magic wielder?" he asked, leaning forward and resting his hand on my shoulder, giving it a slight squeeze.

There it was. That's what he wanted, and I knew it. The pressure on my shoulder grew a little more, but wasn't painful or intimidating. Regardless, he'd managed to make me extremely uncomfortable.

"I'm sorry, Mr. Grandville. I'm not comfortable with that. My magic isn't for parlor tricks, and I'm not in the wish-granting business. I hope you understand," I answered, trying to stay as diplomatic as possible while still standing my ground.

There was an unmistakable flash of anger in his eyes, a slip of the mask he'd put on for me, before it disappeared, and the mask slid back into place. His hand crept down my arm until his thumb was brushing a seductive trail down the bare flesh exposed by my T-shirt. Leaning in a little, his eyes dipped to my chest. He was so close, I could smell the scotch on his breath. The man was too close for comfort, and when his eyes focused on my lips, I had no doubt what he was trying to do. I wasn't about to have any part of it.

Nope. Nopity nope.

I shot up out of the chair like a fire had been lit under my ass.

"Mr. Grandville, I'm sorry, but no. You're a married man, and I'm your employee. This is inappropriate on multiple levels, and I'm not that kind of girl."

I spun and exited the room before he could say anything more. The door shut a little harder than I intended, slamming loudly as I bolted for the safety of my room. I sped only to stop a few feet shy of the door. The sound of glass shattering sounded from Mr. Grandville's office. It would appear the man had a bit of a temper to top it all off.

When I was finally tucked safely inside the confines of my bedroom, I could finally breathe a sigh of relief to be away from that man. He was a skilled actor, which had become very clear when I'd witnessed the slip of his charming mask.

I focused on my door, half expecting the pissed warlock to come charging through it, and waved my hand in front of it. The air shimmered for a second before it settled into a secure calm. There was no way anyone was going to be coming through it without an invitation again.

Nearly twenty minutes later, the door downstairs slammed shut. Not long after, I heard Mrs. Grandville's telltale heels clicking against the hardwood floors. Curiosity was getting the better of me. My magic surged forth, allowing me to watch everything that was happening in the hallway without ever moving from my bed. No one would even know I was watching.

When I heard the door to Mr. Grandville's office open, I withdrew. Would he tell her what happened? Would he twist reality to make himself look like the victim? The man made my skin crawl, and now I knew it was for a good reason. My magic refused to be quieted, though. I reinforced the barrier around my room once again, just to be sure. I kept my ears alert, waiting for one of them to approach my door.

That night, it took me a long while to settle down enough for sleep to take me. Gabriel's words were still playing in my head over and again when I succumbed.

⌁

A WARM SUMMER breeze caressed my bare flesh. I glanced down at myself, and instead of my black pants and purple T-shirt, I was wearing a nearly skin-tight black dress that barely covered my butt. It wasn't something I would usually wear, like ever, but I had to admit I was liking what it was doing for my figure. No mirror was needed to know that I looked smoking hot.

"I'm glad you could finally join me. I was beginning to worry you wouldn't show tonight," a deep voice boomed behind me.

I turned to see Gabriel, standing with nothing on besides his low-slung black pants. The muscular V of his torso drew my eye.

"Where are we?" I asked, noting the grandeur of the bedroom surrounding us.

A large four poster bed stood against the wall with a leather chaise lounge at the foot of it. Its oxblood color drew the eye, standing in stark contrast to the white-and-gold bed with black-stained wood.

"This is my home. I hope you don't mind that I steered us here. I wanted to be somewhere a little more private and comfortable. If it bothers you, we can go somewhere else," he offered.

"No, this is fine. I was just curious. There are so many things I want to ask right now. Like, is this a dream? Is this what you were talking about when you said we'd met before?"

He nodded.

"I . . . I don't know what to say. This is so strange, but there's something about this, about you, that feels right."

He crossed to me in an instant, moving faster than humanly possible, but he wasn't a human, and all of this was real life.

"Then don't say anything. Just feel," Gabriel purred, closing the distance between us and taking me in his arms.

His lips crashed down on mine, melding together and creating something bigger than either of us. So often I was reserved and careful about my actions, but not with Gabriel. With him, I felt like I didn't have to think. I could just live and let whatever happened be.

My lips moved against his as though we'd done this dance a million times before. His tongue brushed along the seam of my mouth, begging entrance. I was helpless to do anything but surrender to him. I'd never wanted a man more than I wanted him in that moment.

In a quick swoop, Gabriel cradled me against his chest and crossed to the bed. He tossed me down into the fluffy duvet that billowed around me.

He stood at the edge of the bed with his stare fixed on the apex of my thighs. My core clenched at the thought of him touching me there. Gabriel's fingers trailed up the bare skin of my legs, peaking over my knee and skimming closer. I wiggled, trying to ease the ache of need that was driving me into a frenzy.

"I don't think I've ever seen such a beautiful sight, love. I can smell how much you want me."

His words were like throwing gasoline on an already raging inferno. I bit my lip to stop myself from trembling with need.

"Please, Gabriel," I moaned, pushing myself up.

I was about to shift around and grab for the button on his pants, but Gabriel held his hand up.

"Let me have the honors, desert rose. I want to taste you."

I shivered at his words and lay back into the cloud of a bed. He followed me, climbing over top of me and shoving my dress up to expose my throbbing bare sex.

"So wet," he groaned, gliding his finger through my soaked folds.

My legs shook and my breath came in short pants. With sure strokes, Gabriel circled my clit, never touching it directly, yet getting closer with each pass.

"Oh gods," I moaned, squirming closer.

"That's right, love. I want to hear how much you need me. Don't hold back," he said, shoving my legs wide and leaving me completely exposed.

His touch was cool, and yet he was setting me on fire everywhere he touched. Grabbing my waist, he dragged me to the edge of the bed and dropped to his knees, throwing each leg over his shoulders. The second his mouth touched my needy core, I almost detonated.

My fingers curled into his hair, tugging and twitching as he lapped up my juices like a fine wine. Pressure built inside and climbed higher and higher. Gabriel plunged his blunt finger into my molten depths, hitting that spot deep inside that made me squeeze around him tightly. I was close.

Gabe worked his fingers in and out of me at a feverish pace, while his tongue teased my swollen nub relentlessly. I was nearing my peak.

"Yes! Right there," I moaned.

It spurred Gabe on. He pushed deeper, hitting the end in a sweet mix of pleasure and pain. Then I was there, standing on the edge, and I jumped, riding the waves of my orgasm.

"Gabriel! Oh my . . . Fuck!" I cried, shattering around his thick digit.

He curled his finger, hitting it just right, and that's when I was fairly certain I saw actual stars. I squeezed my eyes shut tight, and every muscle seemed to tense up with the orgasm. He didn't stop, not until every aftershock and spasm had ceased. My heart pounded, and I let out a long languid sigh.

"Whoa."

He smirked, showing off those sexy dimples, and the tips of his fangs peeked out below his upper lip. Before he could say anything, I felt like I was falling, and then I was torn away from Gabriel and his bed and was back in my own.

My alarm blared on the side table, waking me from the most earth shatteringly delicious dream I'd had in a while. My legs still felt weak, like it had all been real, when I went to stand from the bed. I had a whole new set of questions to ask when I met Gabriel later that afternoon.

CHAPTER 8

GABRIEL

*S*unlight streamed in through the window, warming my skin. I stretched out, still smelling Alina's intoxicating scent on my sheets. The dreams were getting more real all the time. God, she was stunning. I kept replaying the way she'd squirmed against me or ground herself against my mouth harder when I was doing it exactly how she wanted me to.

How was I going to be expected to behave myself after such a night? And in front of children, no less! It was going to be a challenge. I climbed out of bed and went in search of Lorenzo. He needed to know that plans had changed, because now that I'd found Alina, there was no way I was walking away from her.

My throat ached with thirst, and I knew I had to feed before I went to meet her. I'd have to make a stop at Sanguine Elixirs to quench the hunger. It wasn't anything like drinking straight from the source, but it got the job done in a pinch. I ventured downstairs to begin my day and keep busy until it was time to meet my lovely Alina.

It was becoming all too clear while I was running around taking care of the to-do list before my date with Alina that I was acting like a lovesick pup. Never in my wildest dreams did I believe I'd be *that guy*. However, the time had come, and the fact was that I no longer gave a fuck about being that guy. If I had her, nothing else mattered. All I had to do was get through the next few hours until I could see her again.

By the time two o'clock rolled around, I'd already been at the park for twenty minutes, just in case she showed up early. I'd even resorted to pacing at one point. A million scenarios played out in my head about how things would be after I made sure the memory of last night stuck with her. Every single scenario evaporated the moment I heard her voice approaching.

Alina was assuring the children they would have a good time before they rounded the corner and strode into the park.

"It'll be fine, Tabby. It's not like I'm taking you to the dentist to have your teeth pulled. It's just the park," Alina told her young charge as they made their way toward the rink.

The girl rolled her eyes at Alina, who was obliviously searching around for me. She spied me standing by the ice rink. Her cheeks instantly heated, and her luscious mouth lifted into a lazy grin.

My mouth went dry like I'd run a marathon and the butterflies felt as though they'd morphed into pterodactyls. Alina ushered the children off to the benches by the rink, keeping a close eye on them before approaching me. I closed my mind, making sure I wouldn't trespass on any private thoughts. I never wanted her to feel like she had to protect herself against me.

"Hey, um, I'll be right back. I need to help them get their skates on," she added, holding up two pairs of child-sized ice skates.

She turned and sauntered over to a bench where her young charges were busy taking their shoes off. Her perfect round ass swayed with each step. God, how I wanted to bite it and watch it turn a lovely shade of pink while her luscious lips wrapped around my cock, milking me to completion.

Apples, trees, rocks. I was thinking of anything I could to keep my thoughts from straying to the night before. The last thing I needed was to be rocking a raging boner in the middle of a semi-crowded park and watching young kids ice skating. Alina laced up their skates like she'd done it a hundred times and ushered them out onto the ice. Making her way to me, she tucked her hair behind her ears nervously.

"Hi," she said shyly, chewing on her bottom lip like she had the night before when she'd come apart under my touch.

"I want to bite that lip," I said, breaking the tension and moving in to kiss her. I couldn't help myself.

She didn't resist me in the least. Her mouth sought out mine, and her arms snaked around my neck as she tugged me closer. The kiss was quick, but full of emotions and need we were both feeling. It was everything. It was lust, excitement, uncertainty, and love, though Alina didn't need to know about that last part, at least not yet.

"This is all real, isn't it?" she whispered, pulling back a little, though staying close enough that our bodies were always touching.

"As real as it gets, love," I replied, my thumb brushing over her bottom lip.

She shivered and turned her head, watching the kids. I followed her stare and spotted the children making careful and wobbly laps around the rink. I straightened slightly, remembering we were in public. I was more than willing to give everyone a show, but Alina was mine, and I preferred her goods remained mine to be unwrapped and savored in private.

"I really should be keeping an eye on them," she mused, pulling away from me and leading the way to a bench by the rink.

I followed behind, noting the sparkle in her eye when she watched the Grandville children. It wasn't like a mother watching her young— that was too intimate for what this was. This was more like a woman respecting the great responsibility she'd been given.

"How long have you been caring for them?" I asked, breaking the charged silence that had formed.

"Not long. Only about a week. What about you? How long have you been here?"

I shrugged. "Not much longer than you. I moved away to figure out who I was away from my old life. I always felt like an outcast, searching for something more than I should be able to want. It only occurred to me a few days ago that maybe what I was looking for all along was right here. It was you."

Alina's lips parted at my unexpected confession, and I heard her heart rate kick up, but she didn't smell afraid, so I pressed my luck.

"I know you have a lot of questions. I would, too, if I were you. Last night was . . . amazing, to say the least. It's crazy and sudden, but there's a connection here I never even knew was possible. I'm not ready to give you up."

Alina had turned to face me squarely during my confession. Her face was an unreadable mask, and I wanted more than anything to know exactly what she was thinking.

"This is unlike anything I've ever experienced before. It's like my soul was calling out for something more and you answered," I added.

"I couldn't have described it better myself," she answered.

I opened my mouth to say more, but the sound of children yelling captured our attention before I could.

"Freaks!" a group of children called, cornering the Grandville children on the far side of the ice.

There looked to be five children to their two, shoving them and telling them they needed to get off their rink.

"Oh gods!" Alina exclaimed, jumping up.

"It's okay, I've got this." I stopped her and started for the ice rink.

"Are you sure?" she asked, uncertain.

I nodded and strode right for the group of bullies, carefully minding the ice. A girl with curly red hair threw a rock at the young boy, missing his face by barely an inch. Someone was going to get hurt.

"Hey!" I roared, closing the distance between the bench and where they had the children corralled. "What's going on?"

The bullies saw me and scattered like roaches before I could reach them at a human pace. Sometimes I really hated the no-humans-in-the-loop rule. It made making an example of people more difficult than it needed to be.

The girl was holding her brother's hand, and he was sniffling and trying not to cry like I knew he really wanted to.

"Are you guys okay?" I asked, dropping to my knees in front of them.

They watched me nervously, not answering me. My eyes surveyed every inch of them, searching for any sign of injury.

"It's okay, Tabby, Neil. He's my friend," Alina said from right behind me.

Alina must've been following right behind me. Tabby eyed Alina over my shoulder and wiped a tiny tear from her cheek.

"We're fine. I told you this was a bad idea," she snarled, anger warring with big fat tears that were beginning to well up in her eyes.

"Let me tell you something. I want you to remember that the problem is with them. Anyone who would single out someone else or pick on them like those kids, they're busy trying to point the finger at everyone else so no one sees how weird or broken they are. You're perfect the way you are and don't you dare listen to something those little asswipes said," I explained,

"Gabriel! Language, they're just children,"

I lifted a shoulder only half apologetically.

"How about we grab some hot cocoa? That fixes everything," I offered.

I'd never actually drunk the stuff, never having needed to. Although, as a cultural staple, who was I to tell about a billion people they were wrong?

"I want extra chocolate!" Neil yelled, wiping his nose on the arm of his jacket.

"Great choice! What about you, Tabby? What kind do you want?"

"Mother wouldn't approve."

"Well, some rules are meant to be broken," I replied with a wink.

I started for the Danzan Park concession stand and had only made it about fifteen feet when Tabby murmured, "With marshmallows."

In a few short moments, I was back with steaming cups in hand.

"Wow!" Neil exclaimed, blowing into the opening.

Alina took the spot directly next to me, across from the kids, and wrapped her arms around my shoulders.

Leaning in close, she whispered, "That was a really sweet thing you did for them. Thank you."

"If they were mine, I'd hope someone would do the same for them. It's only right."

We spent another hour chatting and making jokes. Little by little the kids came out of their shells, talking with a bit more ease and interacting more than they had when I first saw them. I could tell Alina was noticing the change too.

When the day was over, none of us wanted it to end. Reluctantly, I let my woman go, back to finish her duties with the promise she'd message me to see her later that evening. The night before, we'd shared a dream. Tonight, I was hoping to finally have a taste of the real deal. Watching her leave with Tabby and Neil, my eyes were glued to her ass as it swayed with perfect grace. It was going to be a painful wait.

With luck, I'd managed to get an audience with the local outlaw crew, Swords of the Infernal Night Motorcycle Club, or SIN, as they were more aptly called. Enzo was waiting for me in a parking spot across from the park. As soon as I climbed into the rear seat, he turned.

"They sent us a location. It's some ways out of town boundaries in an abandoned gas station. Are you sure you want to meet with them? It's not too late to back out," he pleaded.

I knew he didn't like the sort I tended to work with. Grudges lasted centuries, and having the right friends in the right places could make or break a man. I had no intention of letting them break me, so SIN was going to help me stack my deck.

CHAPTER 9

ALINA

Gabriel wasn't at all what I'd expected. As a vampire, I'd thought he'd be dark and broody, and maybe he was sometimes, but he was also caring and compassionate. He'd been the first one to try to cheer up the kids and bring them out of themselves, more than I'd been able to accomplish in a week. I wondered what his past was like, but more than anything, I wanted time for him to volunteer everything there was to know about him.

Still on cloud nine when we arrived back home, I wasn't expecting to be ambushed as soon as I marched through the door.

"Tabitha! Cornelius! To your room now!" Mrs. Grandville roared, as soon as I shut the door behind us.

"What's going on?" I asked, wide-eyed and confused by her anger.

The kids didn't hesitate and bolted for the stairs to hide in their rooms. As soon as they disappeared from view, Mrs. Grandville rounded on me.

"What's going on is you going against my expressed wishes and cavorting with a disgusting bloodsucker in front of my children like a common whore! Who the hell are you to make such a decision? What else have you been doing in front of them or subjecting them to? Hmm?"

Red flags went up like flares from a sinking ship. I didn't know what to say, but Mrs. Grandville was only just getting started.

"Where were you?" Mrs. Grandville roared, stomping toward me from the living area.

"I went into town. Figured if I was going to be living here, I needed to know the town and meet some new people."

"And did you?"

"Yeah, the town's lovely. The rink was—"

"I'm not talking about the damn rink, you trollop! I'm talking about that disgusting bloodsucker you were seen cavorting with."

She must've seen the shock on my face.

"Yes, I know all about it. There's nothing you could do in this town that I wouldn't know about, and in this house, everything you do, even off the clock, is subject to scrutiny. If you like working here, then I would suggest choosing very carefully those you wish to associate with, not that you should have time for such a waste."

I was taken aback. The only person I'd ever had tell me who I could or could not be friends with was my father when I'd brought my first boyfriend home. It hadn't worked out well for my father, but an employer? I didn't even know what to say. I was stunned into silence. Was a job worth dealing with this sort of bullshit? My gut said hell no.

"Look, I know you're probably used to telling the children how to live, and I can appreciate the care you have to take to ensure you have people you can trust working with your children, but—"

"You are not to see him again. Ever. Have I made myself clear?" Mrs. Grandville interjected.

"No," I said simply.

"Excuse me?" she howled.

"I said no. You can tell me who the children can be around. You can tell me where they can go and what they can do. Hell, you can even tell me what I'm allowed to do when I'm on the clock. There is no fucking way you're going to tell me who I can see on my own time, which, by the way, I am taking back. Saturdays and Sundays were in my contract. If you don't like my terms, then we can end this conversation right here. I'm not your child, and you have no right to dictate my life," I forced out, my voice beginning to tremble with anger as I slammed my point home.

Her eyes narrowed. "You'd sacrifice your job for a man you just met? You really are clueless."

"I'm not clueless. I know who he is and what he is. I just won't let someone else's prejudices dictate my feelings toward a man I love."

"You think you've got what it takes to make it on your own? I can tell you from firsthand experience, you don't have what it takes. Give it time. You'll see I'm right. If I have to make my point again, you're finished," Mrs. Grandville sneered, turning and striding away from me with only the angry clicks of her heels to keep me company.

CHAPTER 10

ALINA

*L*ater that evening, my phone buzzed. Gabriel's name lit up the front of my phone. I tried to ignore the damned butterflies and giddy feelings just the mere idea of him created, but there was no use.

Meet me outside your gate at 11:30.

I replied with a smiley face and a thumbs up emoji. Glancing at the clock, I saw it was only just barely after eight in the evening. I flopped back and turned on the small TV, losing myself in old reruns of crime shows.

Grabbing a gray sweater dress from my closet, I paired it with some black tights and my knee-high boots to complete the look. It was going to be subtly sexy without being over the top and in your face. Though I was sure there was only one way tonight could go, and that wouldn't involve clothes.

The time to leave arrived, and I released the wards to my room. Creeping out, I listened carefully. All was quiet, but I wasn't taking any risks of getting caught this time. Bringing the image of the front of the Grandvilles' house to the forefront of my mind, I focused and unleashed the magic within. The sound of wind filled my ears, though I knew no one else could hear it. Closing my eyes, I snapped my fingers and let the howling wind take me. When I opened them again, I was standing outside the house on the front porch.

"I was almost worried you were going to leave me hanging," Gabriel teased from the curb.

"You think I'd do that to you?" I joked, sauntering toward him.

Gabriel's Lexus was parked on the roadside, while he held the passenger door open for me.

"I said almost, love. Now, I'm taking you somewhere special."

An excited chill ran through me.

"Where are we going?" I asked, slipping into the passenger seat and fastening the seatbelt.

"Telling you would ruin the surprise. My lips are sealed. You'll just have to wait and see," he said, shutting my door and moving around to the driver's side. He was practically vibrating with excitement.

The car was already running, and the leather seats were smooth like velvet. Without wasting another precious second, Gabriel took off, leisurely stroking my thigh as I wished it was somewhere more intimate.

I kept thinking about what Mrs. Grandville had said about Gabriel being a killer. I didn't doubt he'd killed in his long life. He was a vampire, and it sort of came with the territory. He was also from a different time, when life was snuffed out easier than it was now, with medical interventions. None of that mattered to me, though, because I knew deep down to my bones that he would never hurt me. He had his secrets, and one day, I hoped he would feel comfortable enough to share them with me, but in the meantime, I had a secret of my own that he deserved to know.

"I'm a Marid djinn," I blurted.

Gabe's head swiveled in my direction. "I know, love."

"You do?"

He nodded, tapping his temple. "You're a loud thinker sometimes. I knew you'd tell me when you were ready, and I didn't want to pry."

"Oh. I was just thinking that I didn't want there to be any more secrets between us. I don't like people knowing what I am. It can get dangerous for me, for my family, or the race as a whole."

"You're right to be afraid, but you don't ever need to fear me. Your secret is safe, but I have to ask. Is it true what they say about a Marid's power being derived from an amulet?"

I had to giggle. There were so many myths surrounding my kind that some of them were just crazy.

"Yes and no. My power comes from within myself, but it's tethered to my opal," I explained, pulling the necklace out. "If someone were ever to steal my necklace, they could force me to do anything they wished. I would no longer be in control of what I do. Worse, they could imprison me inside it for all of eternity if they wanted to."

"You'd be their slave?" he asked, his jaw flexing as he gritted his teeth angrily.

"Yes, essentially," I answered, noting the white forming on his knuckles. "You're angry. Why?"

Gabriel sighed warily.

"Once upon a time, I knew the sting of a master's whip. I bear the scars as a reminder. The practice incites me to violence, so God help the poor bastard who ever tries to take what's mine."

"Yours?" I asked, grinning like a fool, because the thought of this man being so protective and possessive of me made me want him even more.

"Yes. You've been mine since the moment you walked into my dream and showed me there was more to life than death and decay, that I no longer needed to be a shadow merely existing," he said, laying his cool hand on my thigh.

With the barest of touches, my panties were already soaked. He could surely feel the charged tension between us. It was so thick you could've cut it with a knife.

Right as I was about to throw all caution to the wind and jump on him, the car rolled to a stop in front of a grand mansion.

"We're here," Gabriel announced, giving me a devilish wink and climbing out of the car.

Moving around the vehicle, Gabriel opened the door for me and ushered me out of the car.

"Welcome to my home."

CHAPTER 11

GABRIEL

*a*lina's eyes widened as she took in the estate.

"This . . . is yours?" she said, stepping into my side and wrapping her arms around my waist.

"It is now. My inheritance, if you will. It's a long story, and I don't want to bore you, so let's take this inside and get to know each other a little better. We have a private dinner waiting. What do you say? Join me?"

A bright smile graced her full lips, and she slipped her hand into mine.

"That sounds wonderful," she replied.

Stepping inside, she froze, and her eyes widened as she took in the grandeur of the foyer and the inviting marble staircase.

"This is like something out of a fairy tale," she murmured, peeking at me over her shoulder as she went.

Her eyes traveled over me hungrily, and I wanted nothing more than to throw her over my shoulder and whisk her upstairs to spend the evening with her riding my cock. She deserved better than that. Alina deserved a gentleman, though if she tested my self-control much more, I'd throw caution to the wind and do as I pleased.

"The dining room is this way," I announced, my hand settling on her lower back as I ushered her deeper into my domain.

As expected, Enzo had put together an elegant meal which was already laid out, steaming, and waiting for us. Candles were a nice touch, aided by the dim recessed lighting to set the perfect mood.

"Wow, this is . . . just wow. It smells so good," Alina remarked, taking a tentative step forward and then another.

Taking a seat, she dug right in, trying everything there was to offer. We spoke animatedly as she ate, learning more about one another. When she'd had her fill, Alina made another kind of hunger known.

Pushing myself up, I strode around the table with the grace of a cat stalking its prey. Alina's bright eyes tracked me the entire journey. The flutter of her heart picking up pace, and her pheromones flooding the air, made my dick strain almost painfully against its confines. I wanted nothing more than to lose myself in her, but all in good time.

Kneeling beside Alina, I gazed up at her, struck by her beauty that radiated from the inside out.

As I brushed the back of my fingers over her bronzed complexion, she leaned into my touch.

"Alina, I've been alive for a very long time, and never once have I faced anything as scary as the idea of letting you know the real me, letting you love me. The way I feel—it's big, and I don't know what tomorrow holds, nor can I make any promises. But what do you say, desert rose? Will you let go of everything you believe and step into the unknown with me?" I asked, pushing up to my full height and extending an inviting hand to her.

Eyeing my hand, Alina bit into her bottom lip contemplatively before reaching out and accepting my invitation.

Good girl.

With a quick yet gentle tug, I pulled her into my arms. Her lithe frame fit perfectly against my own, as though she was made just for me. Holding tightly around my neck, she lifted her cognac gaze to lock with my own. I turned, heading for the stairs, and let loose my restraint. I surpassed human capabilities as I bolted up the stairs toward my bedroom with Alina cradled carefully in my arms.

Within the span of a second, we'd entered my room, and I was laying her down on my bed. Stepping back to give her a moment to adjust, I popped the top button of my shirt free and untucked it as I got comfortable. Alina pushed up to her feet and closed the short distance between us, but unsteadily fell into me instead.

"I'm so sorry. I thought I was okay, and then the room started to spin," she said, gathering fistfuls of my shirt into her dainty hands to anchor her.

My hands came to rest on her hips, kneading the soft flesh through her top.

"There's nothing to be sorry for. The mistake was my own. It can be disorienting at first, but you should be fine. No long-term effects," I said apologetically.

As she shifted her weight, the length of her brushed over mine, and Alina's breath caught, though she wouldn't meet my gaze head on. Shaky, nimble fingers released their hold on me and moved to the buttons of my shirt. Sliding my hand up the side of her, I brought it to rest on the side of her neck, tipping her face toward me.

"Are you afraid of me?" I asked, my fangs lengthening as I inhaled her spicy, sweet scent.

Her eyes met mine and darkened with desire.

"No. I should be scared, but the only thing I feel with you is safe. I know what you are, Gabriel Doyle, and I know that you'd never hurt me. The man you were is not the man you are now, the man I fell in love with and thought for so long was just a figment of my imagination. I need to know this is real, Gabriel. Please?" she asked, her voice so raw and genuine that I had to obey.

"Your wish is my command, darling."

Gripping her tightly, I lifted her as her legs locked around my waist securely. Her lips descended on mine with a hunger that could rival a starving man's. There was no easing into it. We were both laying it all out and giving ourselves to each other completely.

Sweet and innocent was the personality she portrayed to the world, but behind a closed bedroom door, that fell away. Alina took control, tearing my shirt open and shoving it down my arms and out of her way.

Pushing her sweater up her slender torso, I tugged it over her head and tossed it to the floor. Alina gyrated her hips, bumping against my throbbing erection just right. God, I couldn't wait to be inside her. Nipping at my bottom lip, she pulled back with a sly grin. Oh, she knew exactly what she was doing to me.

With a quick snap of my fingers, her bra joined the growing pile of clothes littering my bedroom floor. As I lowered her to the bed, her hands went instantly to my belt, unfastening it and pulling it off. Popping the button on my slacks, she shoved them down, along with my briefs, freeing me to seek the warm, wet sanctuary of her waiting lips. Her hand gripped my shaft firmly, making long strokes as her cheeks hollowed and her tongue ran up and down me. Boldly, she stared up at me the whole time, watching raptly for my reaction. Every twitch and groan drove her harder. Fisting her hair, I pushed deeper, slamming into the back of her throat before pulling her free of me.

"I need to be inside of you," I growled, pulling her to her feet and capturing her lips, relishing her sweet taste with a hint of myself.

It was an aphrodisiac to know in some small way she carried my scent. In that moment, Alina decided it was time for her to seize control of the situation. I stepped out of the pants and kicked them aside before Alina planted her hand in the center of my chest, spinning me around and pushing me back toward the bed. I fell backward onto my bed while Alina slid her tights down her long legs. I sat up, reaching across the distance between us, and tore her purple lace panties from her body, leaving her bare for my eyes to feast upon.

"Patience, Gabriel. Haven't you heard good things come to those who wait?" she teased, climbing onto the bed and kneeling between my legs.

"I've been very patient, waiting as long as I have. If you tease me much more, I'm not sure I'll be able to stop myself from fucking you the way you need," I replied, my voice husky with lust.

Climbing up me, Alina nipped at my belly and chest, her legs settling on each side of me so she was straddling me. She hovered over my cock, lowering herself just enough to slicken the head.

"Is that a promise?" she asked coyly.

Narrowing my gaze at her, I grinned slyly as I gripped her hips and flexed, driving home and burying myself to the hilt in her molten pussy. She gasped, squeezing her walls around me, and let out a long moan as she adjusted. After a moment, she began to move, pushing up and sinking back down in tantalizingly slow rhythm.

Up, down, rock forward until I bottomed out.

Her pace was picking up quickly as I glided through her wet folds with ease. Alina's perfect round breasts bounced in my face mesmerizingly. They filled my palms as I brought her pinkish-brown nipple to my lips and latched on. Her head fell back as she pushed into me. Throaty cries filled my room as she began riding me harder. The thudding of her heartbeat filled my ears, and I could feel the needy ache low in my belly as she drove me closer to my end.

Alina's silky walls quivered, tightening ever so slightly, and I knew she was close to her end too. Pressure was building low in my belly with each gyration of her hips.

"Gabriel, oh yeah. Right there," she cried, impaling herself on my cock harder.

Shooting up to a sitting position, I held her tightly against me as she shattered, pushing me over the edge and igniting the spiral of my own orgasm. Pleasure jolted through me with a force that took my breath away. Thick ropes of my seed exploded from me, filling her to the brim and spilling out. Alina's nails raked down my shoulders as she pulsed around me, drawing each spasm of my orgasm out. Without thinking, I bit down, just below her collarbone. Alina's rich blood filled my mouth as my tongue lapped at the bite.

"Oh fuck. Fuck, yes. Gabriel!" she screamed in ecstasy, clutching my head to her.

I took pull after pull of the sweet liquid until I came back to myself and leaned back. I pushed my thumb onto the sharp point of my fang until it broke the surface and blood welled up. Smearing it onto the punctures, I watched the skin knit back together, staunching the bleeding.

Alina and I fell onto the bed, panting from the exertion. Her sweat-slickened body wrapped around mine.

"That was . . . wow," she murmured.

"Mmmm," I grunted, tugging her closer.

My cock twitched, hardening as the images of her riding me replayed.

"I don't think I'll ever tire of this," I confessed, rolling over her until I was seated and aligned between her legs.

She pulled my head down to hers, kissing me with renewed passion. We made love over and again, until the sun's rays began to peek over the horizon. I drove Alina back to the Grandvilles', wishing I could whisk her back to my home and keep her there forever, but she'd told me what had happened earlier. She wanted to face it head on and let the chips fall where they may. When I pulled up next to the curb, I made her promise to text or call that evening to tell me how things went. Well-fucked was a sexy look on her as she strode up the porch and slipped into the Grandvilles' home and out of sight.

Returning home, I went to open the door when the door knob turned and the door swung open before I could touch it.

I froze.

No one was there, but the door still hung open. Stepping inside, I focused on the door and just as unexpectedly, it slammed shut. Digging my keys out of my pockets, I held them in the palm of my hand and less than ten seconds later, they rose and hung themselves on the key hook in the kitchen.

Well, this is an interesting development, I thought.

Alina had shared her magic with me when I'd drunk from her. The possibilities seemed endless; however, I'd need to tell her to be more careful in the future about who she let drink from her, not that I thought I'd be letting that happen any time soon.

The rest of the day was spent testing the magic. Late in the afternoon, I braved sleep and hoped Alina was sleeping, too. Even though I'd just spent the night with her, I missed her like it had been years. Her place was by my side. Hours passed as I waited, but she never came.

Something was wrong, so very wrong.

CHAPTER 12

ALINA

The house was dark by the time I returned. My cheeks were flushed with excitement. Sneaking around like what we were doing was dangerous, putting us at risk of being discovered, which gave me an adrenaline rush the likes of which I'd never known. Gabriel was addictive, and when we were together, there was an undeniable connection between the two of us.

I pushed the door open, taking each step carefully so as to not wake anyone inside. Mr. Grandville was the last person I wanted to run in to, not that dealing with Mrs. Grandville was a walk in the park. The smallest squeak from the hinges was the only disturbance.

Slipping into my room, it only took me a second to feel eyes on me and realize I wasn't alone. A dark figure was sitting on the edge of my bed. The person was large enough to be an adult, but not so big as to be a man.

Mrs. Grandville.

With a flick of my fingers, the overhead light came on. I stood there, fidgeting under her scrutinizing glare.

"Where were you?" Mrs. Grandville's calm voice broke the tense silence.

Unable to mask my confused expression, I took a moment to reply.

"I was out seeing a friend." I said simply.

"You were with the vampire again, weren't you?" she asked.

There was an accusing tone in her voice, and her displeasure was more than evident. It was the quiet before the storm. She took my silence as an admission of guilt.

"Of course you were. You smell like sex. I thought I had made myself clear that you were not to see him again?"

The way she spoke about Gabriel lit a fire inside me that couldn't be quelled with any amount of logic. She'd pushed me too far this time.

"You made it abundantly clear I was not to have Gabriel, which is his name, around the children. I have obeyed that request, but what I do in my own personal time away from Tabitha and Neil is my business. I'm sorry, Mrs. Grandville, but you're neither my mother, nor my husband, and therefore have no say in who I am friends with or associate with. Nothing about my relationship with Gabe affects my ability to do my job and keep my professional life and personal lives separate."

"That's where you're wrong. We brought you into our home, entrusted you with our children, provided you with a place to live and a reasonable wage. The way I look at it, you owe us a lot more than the disrespect you've shown time and again. This is my home, and you *will* obey my rules. Have I made myself clear?" she demanded.

Her calm demeanor was more unsettling than her words, which had downright pissed me off. By the end of her rant, I was shaking mad.

"Mrs. Grandville, I left my parents' home because I refused to live my life by someone else's rules. This is no different. I love Gabriel, and he loves me. There's nothing you can say that's going to change that. If you are that opposed to who I see when I'm off the clock that you break into my room and wait for me to come back, then I guess I'll need to find another family. Respect is a two-way street, Mrs. Grandville, and I wish it didn't have to be this way. I care about the children, but I won't give him up, and I won't tolerate anyone disrespecting my privacy."

"Oh, you're going to quit, are you? How rich. You're not going anywhere, and you won't be seeing that demon again, I promise. Recognize this?" she said, dangling my necklace from her long fingers.

The bottom dropped out of my belly, and my blood ran cold. Instantly, my hands went to my neck where my necklace had been sitting securely. My fingers brushed over the cool metal, not understanding what was going on. How did she have my necklace if it was still around my neck? As soon as I thought it, it dawned on me. Somehow, she'd swapped a fake out for my amulet. Pulling it from around my neck, I watched as the glamour wore away to reveal a simple crystal dangling from a silver chain. My blood ran like ice through my veins.

"I thought you might. See? I as good as own you. You don't like my rules or requests? That's fine. You can spend some time alone until you give some serious thought to your actions. Wishes are your specialty, no?"

My mouth went dry instantly. A million questions ran through my head, but the one that stuck out the most was *what happens next?*

The door hinges croaked behind me, and I glanced over my shoulder to spy Mr. Grandville sneaking into the room and cutting off any chance of escape.

"We have some important business to discuss, don't we, Alistair? It would be much easier for everyone if you would be reasonable and cooperative. See? We need money."

I rolled my eyes so hard I could almost see my own ass.

"The Grandvilles were a powerful family once upon a time. We served kings and queens for centuries, and yet, somehow, here we are with nothing more than debt to our names. We can thank Alistair for that."

"Edith, that's enough. You don't know what you're talking about. There were bad investments made, nothing more."

"Do you really think I'm that stupid? Come on, Alistair. You've known me almost twenty years. Have you ever known me to make false accusations? Did you think I'd never discover the *companies* you invested in were shells for escort services? Or the tens of thousands in scotch and high-stakes poker games? You're not the most discreet man."

I could feel Mr. Grandville shift uncomfortably behind me. Not that I could blame him; Edith had a glare that could make an elephant want to shrink to the size of a mouse.

"So what is it that you want from me?" I braved when neither said anything.

"I thought that would've been obvious. You're a wish granter . . . and now you belong to us. Grandvilles used to be wealthy, powerful, respected. That's what I want, what I've earned, what I was promised when I took a philanderer for a husband. Giving me Tabitha and Cornelius's birthright would be a fabulous start," Edith explained.

"And what about me? Are you planning on keeping me as your own personal slave for the rest of your lives?"

There was something in Edith's gaze that confirmed my worst fears.

"Fuck you! You're wasting your time," I spat.

Mr. Grandville's strong fingers gripped my arms. No matter how hard I struggled, he was unmoving. Panic rose within me, and I did the only thing I could think of—I tried to magic my way out of there. My body grew hot, and a scorching wind cut through the room, but I wasn't fast enough.

Mrs. Grandville's words sucked the magic right out of me. It was ancient Sanskrit, the language of the Marids. It was a language I wasn't familiar with, not firsthand anyway. I tried to pull the power up from my core, cursing myself the whole time for not practicing with it more when I'd come of age. However, when I tried to grasp onto something —anything—there was nothing there to answer.

My brain grew foggier by the second, and blackness crept in around the edges of my vision.

And then . . . there was only the empty darkness to keep me company.

CHAPTER 13

GABRIEL

$\mathcal{T}$he hours ticked by as I waited anxiously for Alina's call. I typed out text after text, sending them frantically as I asked where she was, what she was doing, asking her to call me, anything. I needed to do something. Crossing my bedroom to the door, I pulled it open and stuck my head out.

"Enzo!" I hollered down the hallway.

"Yes, sir?" he asked, sleepily wiping the grit from his eyes.

"Can you do something for me?" I asked.

He nodded, smoothing his wild hair down.

"I need you to drive by the Grandville residence and tell me if anything seems off. I can't reach Alina, and I'm beginning to worry something happened to her. It's really just for my peace of mind."

"Yes, sir. I'll leave right away," he answered, disappearing into his bedroom.

He emerged a moment later fully dressed and left on his task. I dialed Alina's number and held the phone to my ear, but it went straight to voicemail.

"Damn it!" I roared, chucking the phone onto the bed.

It took thirty tense and half-panicked minutes for Enzo to return.

"All of the lights were off at the house, sir. There was no sign of the girl. If you'd like, I could inquire after her to the homeowners in the morning?

I shook my head. "No. That won't be necessary, Enzo. Thank you for trying."

He bowed and slunk into his room, shoulders slouched.

The rush of Alina's magic coursing through my veins gave me an idea, but I had to try it quickly. Alina could teleport, and if her powers could work for me, then maybe I could too. I let my eyes fall shut. Focusing on the Grandville home, I pictured myself being there, at the front door. When I opened my eyes again, I was still standing inside my bedroom at Viktor's old estate.

"Fuck!" I exclaimed, slapping my hand against the wall, hard enough to leave a crack in the boards underneath.

It wasn't going to work. A backup plan was exactly what I needed, yet I didn't have one. My thoughts were filled with the worst possible scenarios. Had they kidnapped her? Was she dead already? Had she run away? The worst was not knowing. She professed her love for me when she'd finally remembered everything we'd shared, but had it all been an act?

As soon as daylight broke, I was going to be on the Grandvilles' front steps, demanding answers and to see Alina. If she wanted nothing more to do with me, then I'd hear it from her lips and cross that bridge when we got to it. If it so happened that the Grandvilles were keeping her from me, then I'd kill every last one of them and take back what was mine. They didn't know who they were fucking with, but her disappearance had awakened the beast within, and he was hungry for their blood.

CHAPTER 14

ALINA

I'd heard rumors about my cousin's stay in her stone's prison. She'd come home, thankfully, but she was never the same. Her brother had told us she'd gone mad with the solitude of it, and now, facing it myself, I could see why.

They called this place the Mahashunya for a reason. It was the Great Emptiness. Not even my power would answer my call.

My bare feet were submerged in almost six inches of water. In every direction, for as far as the eye could see, the glassy water's surface was flat and still. The sky was gray and cloudy, yet unchanging.

"Hello?" I yelled, hoping someone else was there with me.

There was no answer. There was nothing.

A chill seeped into my bones and drained the energy from me. I didn't want to move or do anything.

"Anyone? Is there anyone out there? Somebody? Anybody?" I screamed at the top of my lungs, sending up silent prayers that someone would hear my cries.

I couldn't be the only one, I just couldn't.

Not knowing what else to do, I started walking and kept walking until my muscles ached and my feet had long since gone numb. Water had slowly climbed my dress and was weighing me down.

My teeth chattered as my knees buckled under me, sending me

into a splashing heap. The tiny reasonable voice in the back of my head kept telling me to get up and keep going, don't give up, but I couldn't muster a reason to obey. What was the point? No one was there with me, and no one was coming for me. Hell, no one even knew where I was besides the Grandvilles, and they'd put me there.

I'd been so stupid. When they first started acting wrong, I should've left, quit right then and there. I'd let my pride and thirst for independence get the better of me, and look what I had gotten for it. They wanted my compliance. If I refused, there was no telling how long I'd be trapped.

Searching the sky, I tried to locate the source of the light, but there was nothing that stood out. For all I knew, I could've been walking for hours in circles. It seemed like hours, though there was no way to track the passage of time.

Exhaustion was beginning to weigh on me, but how could I sleep? One wrong turn in a deep sleep, and I was done for. I wasn't sure I could die in this prison dimension, but I sure as shit didn't want to find out.

Cupping my hands, I let the water pool in the palms of my hands and lifted it in a quick splash against my face. It was the only thing I could think of to keep myself awake. Droplets fell from the tip of my nose, and tiny rivulets spilled down my cheeks, sending ripples through the steady surface. I watched as they spread, growing larger by the second. They didn't just grow in girth, but in size too. Normally, as ripples grew larger, they began to even out and disappear, however that wasn't happening.

I scrambled to my feet, reenergized by the oddity I was witnessing.

The sickening pull I'd felt the instant I was sent into the prison returned as the world was tipped on its side and darkness swallowed me whole.

When I could finally see again, I was back in my bedroom in the Grandvilles' home. The Grandvilles stood side by side, speaking animatedly in hushed tones.

"What's going on?"

I pushed myself up to a seated position from where I was sprawled out on the bed.

"She's awake," I heard somebody whisper, although I couldn't tell who it was.

My head throbbed. In a rush, everything came back to me. They'd trapped me in the opal prison, which now hung around Mrs. Grandville's slender neck.

"Now that you've had some time to think things through, I imagine you're a little more apt to see reason. Don't you think, Edith?" Mr. Grandville said.

She nodded, lifting the necklace and rubbing the stone between her fingers. There was a steady coldness in her eyes that said she'd send me right back without a second thought the moment I chose not to cooperate. The choice was mine, not that it was even a choice—give them what they wanted or go back to the Mahashunya indefinitely.

"What do you want?" I questioned warily.

My fists knotted into my skirt, wrinkling it.

"My parents owned one of the mansions in Havenwood Heights, where we summered. All of that's gone now, and I want it back. I've earned it a hundred times over, but as you would understand, life's not fair."

"I can give you wealth, which will bring status, but there's nothing I can do to change your ways. All the wealth in the world isn't going to make you a good father for Tabitha and Cornelius, who just want your time and attention, and it's not going to stay if you spend it as irresponsibly as Mrs. Grandville suggested."

Mrs. Grandville stepped forward with fire in her eyes. Her hand whipped out, making a meaty crack as it collided with the side of my face. Hot pain exploded from my cheek, fanning the growing flames of hatred.

"You'll hold your tongue before you find you don't have one," she threatened. "You will do this."

A low creak from outside the bedroom door caught everyone's attention. Mr. Grandville shoved the door open, hand at the ready to dispatch anyone caught eavesdropping.

"Tabitha! Cornelius! What in the devil are you doing out here? I thought you were told to stay in your rooms," he reprimanded.

"Yes, father, but we heard—" Tabitha began, but was cut off by her furious father.

"What you heard is irrelevant! You were given directions and then disobeyed me. Back to your rooms, now! Both of you. I'll be in shortly to hand down your punishment. In the meantime, give this some thought: blood is thicker than water and the world is a cold, cruel place. Especially for children," he spouted, terrorizing his kids in the process.

Fear was written on Tabby and Neil's taut faces. Mrs. Grandville's mouth turned down in a barely discernable frown. It seemed the woman wasn't as heartless as she let on, and if that was the case, there was hope for the kids after all.

"Y-yes, sir," Tabitha muttered, grabbing Cornelius by the hand and dragging him along with her to their room.

Mr. Grandville shut the door, cutting the children off from view. The thought of running was tempting, but I couldn't go anywhere without the opal. It would always pull me right back to it. Mr. Grandville stared over my shoulder at Mrs. Grandville, who stood by the wall behind me.

"What do you say? Think you can manage fifty million? Nothing too large a genie like you can't handle," he said, still not looking at me.

"All right, I'll do it!" I cried. "But I need a few things first."

"We're listening," Mrs. Grandville said behind me.

I'd never done anything on this scale before, but how hard could it be? A wish was a wish, but even then it was complicated.

"Tick, tock, Alina. Your time's about up," Mr. Grandville declared, taking an imposing step toward me.

"Wait!" I shouted, throwing my hands up to keep him at bay. "I-I need the account number where you want it transferred. Unless you want it in cash?"

Mr. Grandville scratched his chin as he contemplated his options. Coming to a decision, he reached into his back pocket and withdrew his checkbook, handing over a blank check.

"Here's the number. Be quick about it. Oh, and I'll be checking to make sure the money's there, so don't get any lofty ideas."

"Don't worry, it will be."

I plucked the check from his hands and scanned the account number, committing it to memory. Magic hummed under my skin, coming alive as I focused on the wish. Normally, I wouldn't attach any strings, but seriously—fuck them. They could keep me locked up for the rest of my life, but I could do everything within my power to make their lives the same hell they'd forced me into.

Pulling my powers to my center, I kept the wish at the front of my mind, picturing it as the transfer was made. The pair had never stipulated that the money had to be untraceable. Mr. and Mrs. Grandville were going to be in for one hell of a rude awakening when the U.S. Treasury discovered they were fifty million dollars short. I couldn't imagine it would take too long for them to trace it, especially with an electronic transfer.

"It's done," I confirmed.

"I'll be the judge of that," Mrs. Grandville voiced, flipping open a laptop that was laying at the foot of my bed.

Her fingers whirred over the keys, pulling the bank account up.

"Fifty million dollars just cleared. She did it," Mrs. Grandville confirmed.

My phone buzzed on the bedside table. Gabriel's name was clear on the screen. How many times had he called? Had he realized I was missing? Would he come looking for me? I liked to think he was my knight in shining black armor that would come to my rescue, but there was no telling. I didn't want to get my hopes up.

I took a step to grab the phone, but Mr. Grandville held a hand up to stop me.

"Not another step," he ordered.

The buzzing stopped, but only momentarily. Gabriel's name flashed across the screen again.

"Oh for fuck's sake!" Mr. Grandville roared, "*Uanescere!*"

The phone disintegrated into dust, littering the table top and carpet. That was as good as my last lifeline. Someone would come looking for me eventually, but who knew where I would be by then or what was waiting for me. My stomach was tied into knots, and I was shocked into silence.

Loud pounding shook the front door of the home. My heart jumped, and I wasn't the only one startled. Mr. Grandville was sweating like an ice-cold can of soda on a hot summer's day, and his eyes were on the verge of bugging out of his head.

"Open the door! Where is she?" Gabriel yelled through the thick wood.

Mr. Grandville shot a wary look at his wife, who appeared just as uneasy as he did. Hiding my elation was the hardest thing I'd ever done. I was giddy with hope that justice would be served.

"I thought you said he wasn't going to be a problem? He was just feeding off the girl, a meaningless tryst?" Mr. Grandville accused.

"I was obviously mistaken," Mrs. Grandville retorted, checking herself over in the oval mirror hanging beside the dresser.

A quick series of slams shook the house as though Gabriel was threatening to tear the whole thing down brick by brick.

"Take care of the girl. I'll get the door before he catches the wrong sort of attention. The last thing we need is an inquisition by the sheriff or the Court," Mrs. Grandville remarked.

Mr. Grandville nodded, holding his hand out to his wife. She took my opal necklace off and dropped the stone into his waiting hand.

I knew what was about to happen before he even began the incantation. I was watching my life happen from outside my body in slow motion. His lips moved, though I didn't hear a sound, and then the pull began. Waves of nausea rolled over me, and in a single blink, I was cast back below the waves.

Back to the Mahashunya.

CHAPTER 15

GABRIEL

I was seeing red as I paced frantically on the front porch of the witches' home. There was no doubt in my mind they were responsible for Alina's disappearance. She wouldn't have no-showed on me herself. That wasn't the sort of woman she was, and despite only knowing each other a short time, I knew she wasn't the type to run away from anything, especially not when she cared as much as she did about the Grandville kids.

The lady of the house opened the door with a dour expression plastered on her magically enhanced face.

"Where's Alina?"

"I'm sure I have no idea what you're talking about."

"Did you know people like me can hear lies in your voice? There's a slight waver and a wrong pitch every time you tell an untruth. I'm calling bullshit. I'm going to be reasonable and give you five seconds to divulge what you know and where she's at before I make a choker out of your entrails."

Mrs. Grandville seemed unfazed by the threat. That was her misstep; she had no idea what I was capable of.

"You think you can come to my home, in front of my family, and make idle threats like an impetuous child? Tell me, Mr. Doyle, do you enjoy being a member of the living? I can promise you, it's well within my power to change that status, should you tempt me. Now, I have no idea where your plaything is. She didn't come home yesterday, or maybe you're trying to cover your own tracks. Maybe you got a little overzealous and accidentally killed the poor woman. Think carefully about that. What story do you think the Court will believe more? That an upstanding member of this town committed an atrocious crime or that a known killer from out of town slipped back into his old ways?" she remarked coldly.

With a roar, I took a step forward, only to be pushed back by the woman's magic. Her palm was open and waiting. My pride had always told me that as a larger specimen, hitting a woman was the cowardly thing to do, but I was on the verge of throwing that sage advice out the window. My fangs were pricking at my gums, threatening to lengthen if my patience was tested any further.

"Is everything all right?" called a bloated middle-aged neighbor, who in his curiosity forgot he was wearing his bathrobe to take out his trash.

"Everything's just fine, Bill! My friend was just leaving," Mrs. Grandville answered, never breaking eye contact with me.

"All right! Just holler if you need anything," the man shouted back, worry lacing every word.

My nostrils flared as I caught a whiff of Alina's scent coming from inside the home. My cheeks stretched into a malicious grin.

"I can smell her," I said simply.

"Oh really? I'm giving the Court a call to come collect you. If you know what's good for you, you'll be gone and far from this town by the time they arrive," Mrs. Grandville spat, slamming the door in my face.

Fuck! Why in the devil would the gods be so cruel to implement the whole invitation rule for vampires? It became rather inconvenient when time was of the essence. Mrs. Grandville was right. If she made the call, knowing I was Viktor Azimov's heir, they wouldn't be lenient, and they very likely wouldn't believe me without an official questioning. By then, Alina could be gone.

Five minutes later, as if on cue, the sheriff's black pickup truck rolled up in front of the house, parking damn near on top of the curb. Sheriff Ric Kasun stepped out of the vehicle, slamming the door a little too hard behind him. He strode around the vehicle and marched right for me. I didn't miss his silver eyes constantly checking the surroundings. I guessed those wolfy instincts never really shut off. He seemed a little informal for the occasion, wearing jeans and a red flannel shirt like some damn lumberjack. The man didn't seem older than forty-five, but I knew he eclipsed that by a few centuries at least.

"Mr. Doyle," he stated, hooking his hands on his hips.

I nodded.

"Can you come over here by the car for a moment? I'd just like to get your side of things before I go talk to the caller."

I complied. If I wanted to help Alina, I needed to keep my head and stay the fuck out of jail.

"Now what can you tell me about what's going on? I received a call that you were trespassing and harassing the residents."

A chuckle escaped before I could quell it.

"I guess all of that's correct. The Grandvilles conveniently forgot to mention that my girlfriend works for them and has gone missing. I came looking for her."

"Missing? When was the last time you saw her?"

"Yesterday morning when she left the home I'm renting for the time being. I've tried to call her close to a hundred times, but there's no answer."

"Did you two have a fight? Would there be any reason you would suspect she's in danger?" he inquired.

I nodded. "She's a rare woman."

"How rare? Be straight with me. I'd prefer to know what I'm walking into and not waste the time to call the Court."

"She's a Marid djinn," I explained.

Sheriff Kasun's eyes widened in surprise. "Oh."

"So you see how this could very easily be more nefarious than a runaway girl?"

He nodded. "I do. However, that being said, it doesn't mean that these folks are keeping your girlfriend locked up. It could be a misunderstanding. Let's talk with them and see if we can get some more information from them and then go from there."

I could see the doubt in his eyes and hear it in his thoughts. He didn't think he'd find Alina inside. He wasn't overly thrilled to be dealing with my kind, but respectably, he put his job first.

"I could smell Alina inside the house. When I told her as much, she called you and slammed the door in my face. Let me be clear, I don't care if I have to bleed the answers I want out of them, but I will be getting those fucking answers."

"Do you think tough talk to the town's sheriff is a good idea? The call we got was about *you*. Not about them, not about your missing girlfriend, but you. If you can't handle yourself, I'll need to cuff you and put you in the back of the car while I go talk to them, which is probably what I should do, if I'm being honest."

Inhaling deeply, I tried to calm my frayed nerves enough to do what I had to in order to get my woman back.

"You won't have to worry about me . . . now. If they're going to jerk us around, then all bets are off."

"That's not how things work here, Doyle. This ain't the Wild West. You need to let us handle this in a way that's best for all involved, if you catch my drift," he said, side-eyeing the neighbors who were nosily creeping onto their porches at the first sight of trouble.

I nodded.

My jaw was clenched so tightly that if I was still human, my teeth would've cracked right in half. Sheriff Kasun took the lead, marching up the paved walkway to the front door. His back was straight and regal, the sort of posture that came with self-pride and only a little edge to make himself seem larger and more intimidating. I stayed behind him, reminding myself that ripping that cunt's throat out wouldn't solve any problems, only create a dozen more.

Ric banged on the door a few times and hooked his hands on his waist as he waited. It's funny how time can bend according to perception. A hundred years had passed in what had seemed like a blink of an eye because there was nothing of value or significance during that time. Alternately, the seconds that ticked by waiting for someone to answer the door stretched into what seemed like an eternity because the woman who had managed to capture my heart and soul depended on me doing right by her. My fists balled at my sides, and my nails dug harshly into the thick flesh of my palms.

Finally, I could see a shadow moving within the home. The door swung in, and to my great surprise, it was not the woman of the house who came to the door. Tabitha came to the door. Her hair was pulled back to reveal her nervous face.

"May I help you?" she asked meekly.

We shared a knowing glance.

"Hi there, I'm Sheriff Ric Kasun. Can you please get your mom for me? I have a few questions to ask her," he said smoothly, pouring on the kind of charm that could easily sway people to do as he wanted.

It was exactly that quality that made the Court appoint him as town guardian and, ultimately, sheriff. I wanted to ask her where Alina was, what had happened to her, but the fear wafting off her made me stop. Something had happened. Tabitha disappeared back inside, leaving the door open a crack.

Rage warred with fear as the seconds ticked by, while we waited for the Grandvilles to open their door. They'd taken Alina from me, and for that, I would make sure they paid dearly.

"If there's so much as a single hair on her head out of place, I swear I will rip them limb from limb and enjoy every second of it," I growled, pacing at the foot of the porch.

"Threats? Really? You're dumber than you look," Sheriff Kasun grumbled.

Quick steps caught my attention as someone rushed to the door. I clenched my fists to stop myself from doing something I'd regret. Witches or not, I knew people who made these folks look like simple card magicians. Not to mention, I could probably rip a throat or two out before they could utter any sort of incantation to stop me. That was the problem with their words—they would never be quite fast enough to stop me.

Mrs. Grandville came to the door, austere superiority written in every movement and glance.

"Sheriff Kasun." She nodded.

There was something in her voice that grated against my last nerve. My jaw clenched. I wanted to barrel through her and find Alina. Fucking curses preventing me from entering without invitation.

"Where is she?" I demanded, leveling the woman with a glare.

Her brows knit together, but otherwise, she remained unfazed.

"Back off, Doyle. Don't make me arrest you for being a nuisance," Kasun said, his eye twitching as the only indication of his apparent dislike of my kind. "Mrs. Grandville, I'm sorry to disturb you, but Mr. Doyle insists that his *friend* was staying here with you as your nanny and she has gone missing. I'm hoping you can offer some insight into the whereabouts of Ms. Anand."

The woman's expression didn't change once, seeming practiced.

"Unfortunately, Ms. Anand is no longer residing with us. She left us late last night without explanation."

"You're lying," I interjected.

"If she were lying, I'd be able to hear it in her voice. You need to calm down and go back to the car. Now. I'm not asking, either," Kasun ordered.

The carefully maintained grip on my rage was beginning to slip. If I wasn't careful, I could reveal something I shouldn't in front of a mostly human crowd, which was beginning to form, curious about the police presence.

"You know what the girl is, Kasun. You know how valuable she could be to the wrong sort of person—"

"Wrong sort? Like you?" Mrs. Grandville remarked, smugly arrogant.

"More like the sort who have no scruples about forced servitude and putting on false airs. I remember your husband's grandfather well. How does it feel to know that you almost had it all and now, you're practically peasants? That's got to rub you the wrong way. Isn't it just convenient a woman who could give you all that just so happened to fall right into your lap. I can't imagine why she'd go missing . . ." The sarcasm dripped from every word as I said it.

Kasun's brows rose at my words, before he regained his sensibilities and pointed toward the patrol car at the curb.

"Mrs. Grandville, I hope you understand that I can't simply take your word for it. Would you mind if I took a look around?"

"Is that really necessary?" she protested weakly.

"You could refuse . . . but then I'd just come back with a warrant when the girl fails to turn up anywhere," he said matter-of-factly.

Kasun was nothing if not professional, even if he was a damn wolf.

"All right then. Be my guest," Mrs. Grandville said, stepping aside and allowing the sheriff into her home.

Something about the whole situation and the family set me on edge. I'd seen people like them once upon a time—the sort who viewed everyone around them as servants to their own greater purpose. My master before I'd been turned had been such a man.

"Kasun?" I said quietly, though I knew even at this distance he could hear me. "Look for Alina's opal necklace. If she's anywhere, it could very well be there."

"Don't you think that's a little extreme?" Kasun pointed out.

"Not in the least. I've seen what humans are capable of inflicting on their own kind, and I've seen what they can do to those they see as different. We may be a different species, but some things don't change that much, no matter the kind."

He nodded, understanding, and disappeared into the house. Mrs. Grandville stood in the doorway after Kasun passed through, casting a glare the likes of which could've killed. There was a smug set to her mouth.

Creaking boards echoed as the man of the house, Mr. Grandville, came to join her at the entrance. He looked me up and down, appraising me.

"What is it you hope to gain from all this? You're making yourself look like a lunatic in front of the whole town. Do you think people will look favorably on your actions? Showing up and issuing threats to upstanding citizens about crimes with no evidence?" he sneered.

"You must be Mr. Grandville. You live up to your reputation."

"I'm sure. And what might that be?" he scoffed.

"A man with very little to offer anyone, especially a woman, but thinks it should all be handed to him on a silver platter. Tell me, Mr. Grandville, was your plan to replace the old ball and chain with the younger model when you came onto the nanny?" I could see the taut lines around Mrs. Grandville's eyes. It seemed I'd struck a nerve. "Or do you just throw it out there and pray someone will want someone as pathetic as you are? Now, let me be clear. I've had far more time on this earth to make friends in high places, much higher than your name will ever get you. All I have to do is snap my fingers, and this town, and more specifically your farce of a family, would be wiped from the pages of history. No one would ever even remember who you were. So here's a bit of advice: know who and what you're playing with before you come to the table. Otherwise, you'll lose your ass every single time until one day, you'll lose far more. And last I checked, you don't have a coven backing you if you fuck up."

"If you're finished," he replied, casting a fleeting glance over his shoulder. "You should know you've made an enemy here today. I'd consider that very carefully."

"Good, I was counting on it. I'm going to make this as clear as I can. If you have Alina, and I have no doubts that you do, I'm going to pick off every branch of your family tree. You'll get to spend the rest of your life looking over your shoulder, and then when you least expect it, I'll come for you."

"Sheriff, I hope everything was as it should be?" Mr. Grandville said loudly, ignoring my threat.

Kasun stepped forward, out of the house, peering at me with uncertainty.

"I didn't find anything to suggest she's in the home, currently," he said, eyeing the neighbors and lowering his voice. "There was a lingering scent that didn't belong to your family. It was recent enough for me to believe the girl was here more recently than you let on. Care to explain that?"

The Grandvilles didn't even flinch.

"No clue, Sheriff, but if you don't mind, we've caused enough of a scene for one day. If you have any more inquiries, I hope you return with a warrant or the Court, because this is feeling an awful lot like a witch hunt."

"Are you not concerned that your nanny is missing?" Kasun asked, scrutinizing the pair even more closely.

"Not really. Seeing what sort of company the girl keeps, it's best not to have one such person around our children. I wish you both the best in your search," Mrs. Grandville replied, stepping back and shutting the door once and for all.

"Fuck!" I roared.

"Not here. Can you follow me?" Kasun asked, his gaze pleading with me.

It was in that moment I knew he was on my side. He'd seen something inside that house that was off, enough that he was doubting what they were telling him.

Kasun turned and started for his truck, waving off the prying eyes who'd gathered.

"Show's over. Everybody can go back inside," he said with an edge.

The sheriff climbed into his truck and slammed the door a little too hard. I followed as he began to drive. He made his way back to the police station too slow for my liking. Time was of the essence.

Pulling into the station parking lot, I came to a stop and was out of the car before Ric had even gotten to his feet.

"What is it? What did you find in the house?"

"Nothing."

"Nothing?"

"Yeah, that's the troubling bit. I could smell her like she'd been there within moments of my arrival. I checked every room in that house, and there wasn't a single trace of her. No clothes, no personal belongings, no necklace, and no Alina. There should've been something, some trail she left behind, even in scent, that would give me a clue where she went, but there wasn't. I don't know what to make of it, but I'm convinced they're hiding something. "

"What's the plan, then?" I asked.

"I'll have to make a few calls. Magic isn't my specialty, and it's going to require someone who could feel something if it was unusual."

"Unusual how?"

"Magic works in mysterious ways. If Alina is a Marid like you say she is, that should leave some kind of imprint on the environment. We need someone who can feel that well enough to be able to find it. Come inside and sit down. I'll give the Luna Coven a call and see if they can be of some assistance."

"Don't involve them. The fewer people who know about what Alina is, the safer she'll be. Besides, I've got someone who I think might be able to help, but I've got to try to reach Alina first. I'll need maybe an hour tops."

CHAPTER 16

ALINA

*M*y entire body felt waterlogged. Where I used to have feet, I now had bloody, beaten remnants. Every muscle in my body hurt from the tensing and contractions as it tried to spasm and stay warm.

Hunger was my constant companion. I'd begun to talk to the growls when they happened. Sometimes it seemed like they answered me, but I knew that was stupid. More than anything, though, I just wanted to hear another person's voice, to know I wasn't alone.

Who knew how long I'd been imprisoned in the Mahashunya? There was no cycle of day to night to keep track. Gabriel's face had begun to fade from memory, too. It no longer had the sharpness of familiarity that it once had. I wondered if my mom and dad knew I was gone. If they did, had they come looking for me?

There'd been so much resentment toward my father before I'd moved, so many fights that now seemed pointless. I'd been stubborn and selfish, unwilling to listen to someone who genuinely knew more about the world and people than I did. I'd figured that one out a little too late.

"Daddy, I don't know if you can hear me, but you were right. I gave my trust to someone who wanted to use me, but you were wrong too. Love, real everlasting love, exists. I don't know if you'd like

Gabriel, but I think you'd be proud that I found someone who cares for me, flaws and all," I whispered, letting the emptiness steal my words away.

Had a Marid ever died in this place? It was a question I'd contemplated close to a thousand times. It would've been easy to end it all. Shame reared its ugly head. Giving up wasn't an option.

My eyes grew heavy, exhaustion threatening to overtake me. I lay back in the water like my dad had taught me how to do as a child when I would float. My hair floated around me like a dark halo. From limb to limb, relaxation eased me into a light sleep. With the water lapping gently at my body, I drifted deeper into the sweet bliss of sleep.

No longer was I trapped inside the Mahashunya. Instead I was standing at the edge of the pool at the base of the falls Gabriel had shown me. Of course, even in my dreams, I was bound to water. A warm breeze blew, carrying a scent I'd become so familiar with since meeting Gabriel Doyle.

I turned and spied him leaning against the trunk of a large tree. He seemed to be waiting for me.

"Alina? Is that really you?" he asked, taking an unsure step forward.

"Yeah, it's me," I croaked, my voice having grown too accustomed to remaining silent with no one to talk to.

Gabriel was to me in an instant, folding me into his arms and crushing me against his chest. He was restrained, trying to be as gentle as he could, but I could tell it was a struggle for him. I clung to him like my life depended on it. I squeezed my eyes shut tightly, relishing the feel of his solid form against my own.

"Where are you? What happened? Tell me how to get to you," he urged, burying his face into my hair and inhaling my scent deeply.

"Are you really here?" I asked, afraid to open my eyes and have him disappear.

He leaned back, taking my face between his hands. With a gentle finger, he tipped my chin up and brushed the hair away from my eyes.

"I'm here, love. I'll never leave your side again. If it means I have to stay here forever, then I'll gladly never wake up."

"This is all a dream?"

He nodded, pointing to the clear night sky where the moon seemed larger than possible.

It shed so much light on the falls and the trees around us that it made it less imposing. I wasn't afraid of being seen and could relax and enjoy the moment.

"I'm in the Mahashunya, and I can't get out. Gabriel, I don't know how much longer I have."

"What's the Mahashunya? Why can't you get out?"

"There are rules. My kind were created by Set, who had grown jealous of Amani and Khalida's power. He stole a feather from Thoth's wing and set it ablaze. He watered the ashes with the Nile River and from that, the first Marids were born. They were too powerful and too greedy to be contained, though. They ravaged the lands and the people began to starve. Set grew angry at his children and decided they could no longer be free. He bound our souls to an amulet. Should we ever grow too bold, the amulet would be our prison. I-I lost my opal, Gabriel. It's gone, and I don't know that I'll ever get it back."

I looked away, feeling the misty beginnings of tears pricking my eyes.

"Listen to me, Alina. Do you trust me?" he asked.

My chin dipped once.

"Then trust me when I say that I'm coming for you. I might not be able to go to the Mahashunya, but I'm working damn hard to bring you back to me. I won't stop until the Grandvilles pay for what they've done and you're here with me. Do you understand? You're mine. Forever and always."

His words were so sure that I wanted to believe every bit of it. I almost did, but there was still the tiny nagging voice in the back of my head that doubted I would ever be saved. I didn't even have magic here, leaving me royally screwed.

Gabriel rested his forehead against mine, rubbing my back soothingly. I'd never grow tired of his touch. I just hoped I got the opportunity to feel it again.

The moon grew dark, and I knew my time was almost over. I was waking up.

"I don't want this moment to end. Hurry, Gabriel."

"Stay with me, love. Don't go yet."

I was torn away before I could tell him the words I'd been wanting to since the moment he'd given me every dream we'd shared: I love you.

My eyes fluttered open. The dull gray sky stared back at me. My fingers and toes were borderline numb, and my skin was so cold to the touch, but not cold enough for hypothermia to set in. As I sat up, my thick hair was weighed down, laden with water. Giving it a hard twist, I wrung it out and got to my feet. Peering out at the flat water stretching in every direction, it all came crashing right back down on me that I was truly alone. My heart sank at the thought.

I didn't know why I hadn't thought of trying to reach out to Gabriel before. The dream walking was one thing, but that he could reach beyond his realm and into a different plane entirely changed the game. There wasn't any more I could offer him. I was too far out of touch with what was going on back home. Hell, I didn't even know how long I'd been gone. Had it been a couple days? Weeks? Months? The Grandvilles could've cut and run, taking the opal along with them, although I could still remember Havenwood Falls, so I doubted I'd tripped the memory wards.

Pondering the seriousness of Gabriel's words, I began my trek. He'd said he'd never leave my side, but there I was, all alone once again. I knew it wasn't his fault. Homesickness. That was what ailed me, though not the home I'd always known with my parents. No, not there. Since moving, I'd found a new safe haven in Gabriel's arms. He was my home now, and I was more homesick than I'd ever been before.

Letting my foot fly, I kicked through the water, sending a spray of droplets and a fine mist soaring. I screamed as loud as I could, unleashing my anger and frustration. There was so much going on in my head that it was too loud to even think clearly. So much rage, sorrow, and uncertainty all rolled into a ball that had been weighing me down. I had to let it out, so I did. Tears streamed down my cheeks, and my throat was raw, mimicking the pain I felt inside. The tears came until my body just wouldn't let me weep anymore.

I was fucked, there was no other way around it. I sniffled and dragged the back of my hand across my face, smearing the wetness on my cheeks more than anything. An ache had begun to form at the base of my skull, throbbing in time with my pounding heart.

"This just keeps getting better, doesn't it?" I sighed sarcastically.

Before I could make another move or utter another word, that familiar tug came rushing back, and I was thrown into darkness as I was dragged back to the world outside of the Mahashunya.

CHAPTER 17

GABRIEL

*R*oman Bishop hadn't anticipated my call coming so soon, but much to my surprise, he answered and he showed . . . twenty minutes after the decided time. Luckily, the Grandvilles hadn't decided to skip town and run for the hills since we'd visited them. Alina had looked so broken when I'd seen her by the falls in our dream walk. It was the first time I'd been able to reach her since she'd disappeared four days prior.

Stepping out of the rear of a black sedan, Roman strode right for Ric and me where we'd parked at the curb across from the Grandville residence.

"You're late," I noted.

"I'm here, aren't I? Let's get this over with. I have plans."

Bishops. Always the smug bastards of the group. That was one thing that hadn't changed since I'd first visited the town. Ric was standing back, silently watching the two of us disinterestedly.

"Tell me again why I've been summoned," Roman demanded.

Ric answered before I could even put together a response. "A Marid girl has been missing for four days now. When I checked the house, her scent lingered like she'd been there just a few moments before, but she wasn't. All personal effects were gone, and the trail is going to go cold if we don't find one specific object. We think the witches who live here might've hidden the girl in an opal necklace."

"And you need me to find this?"

I nodded. "The necklace is bound to the girl's soul. It should have a fairly high concentration of magic contained within it. We need to find her at any cost."

"You want me to find your pet for you. Do I look like a fucking bloodhound?" he asked, stretching his neck from side to side.

"Bishop, if you can't help me, I'm sure I can find someone who will," I pointed out.

"I'll find it. Just hold up your end of our deal when it's time to collect."

"If the two of you are done bickering like schoolgirls, then let's do this," Ric quipped, striding right for the front door.

Sheriff Kasun knocked and stepped back while Roman and I stayed back. Seconds ticked by without any sounds coming from inside. Just as Kasun was about to knock again, the door opened, and Mr. Grandville poked his surprised face out.

"Sheriff, can I help you?"

He didn't spare a single glance for Roman or me.

"You can, actually. Mr. Grandville, we're here to conduct a more thorough search of these premises. Both myself and Mr. Bishop are here on behalf of the Court. I'll need you to gather everyone in the house immediately."

Just as it looked like the man was about to protest, Roman spoke up.

"I'd do as he asked. There's no need to make this any harder than it needs to be," Roman remarked, his eyes narrowing on the English prick.

Mr. Grandville had to be seething internally, but no one doubted Roman would destroy him if Mr. Grandville tried anything. Knowing better than to challenge a Bishop, the lesser mage stepped aside, allowing Ric and Roman entry. I stood just the other side of the threshold, waiting for my invitation.

Mr. Grandville chuckled at my predicament.

"If you know what's good for you, I'd quit toying with me. I'll take any reason to kill you slowly like the *míolra* you are," I threatened.

"I'd listen to him if I were you. I'm not saying I'd let him kill you outright, but there's nothing I could do if he moved faster than me," Sheriff Kasun chimed in.

Mr. Grandville's jaw tightened, and the man was glowering with an intensity that had to hurt.

"Please come in," he gritted.

My lips quirked up.

Smart move, asshole, I thought.

Kasun was standing with his arms crossed, waiting expectantly. Roman stood next to him, waiting for the rest of the household to join us.

"Edith! Tabitha, Cornelius! I need you all down here," Mr. Grandville hollered up the stairs.

All three came quickly, sensing something was off.

"Al? What's going on?" Mrs. Grandville asked, eyes wide as she strode into the room.

She froze as soon as she saw us all. The surprise quickly morphed into outrage.

"What's the meaning of this? I thought we'd made ourselves clear that you were not to come back—"

"Without the Court? That's why I'm here. Roman Bishop. I don't believe we've met," Roman purred, pouring on the charm as he extended his hand to her.

"I know who you are, but what are you doing here?" she hissed, ignoring his hand.

"I'm here on behalf of the Court of the Sun and the Moon to investigate the unknown whereabouts of a Miss Alina Anand. This being her last known address and the residence she was last seen at, we thought we'd stop by. Check things out. I'm sure you understand. We all want the girl found, right?" Roman asked, listening closely for the woman's response, but staying casual, so as to not let on that he was waiting for any indication of a slip up.

Instead of answering, she crossed her arms over her chest and kept her mouth shut. The kids stood next to their mother, wide-eyed and silent. From what I knew of them, they liked Alina a lot. I couldn't fathom either of them having a thing to do with her disappearance.

With the calm of a stalking predator, Roman strode through the house, hands at the ready. There were so many things I could say about the man waiting for the object to *talk to him*. Every time I pictured Alina, I thought better of it and held my tongue. He was being generous enough to help me find her, or at least hope to.

Mr. Grandville took a step to follow him, looking to the sheriff as though asking permission. We all gave Roman room to work, staying a good way back, yet following his every move. No one wanted to miss anything.

He passed through the first floor without taking so much as a second look at anything. Then he began to climb the stairs to the second floor. He'd made it halfway up before he froze. Stepping back down one tread, Roman stomped his foot on the lower step and then the one above it.

There was a completely different tone between the two, and one was certainly hollow. Taking another step down, Roman examined the seam of the step carefully, lifting the board to reveal a hiding hole.

The Grandvilles were silent, eyeing the stash with unreadable expressions. I quietly wondered if they were contemplating how screwed they were, but my need for my woman was stronger. I had to know what was in the hole.

"Well, it's no necklace, but I think we've found the girl's personal items," Roman said, producing a sketch pad with images of my face and a tiny ceramic Ganesh statue.

"Are they hers?" Ric asked.

I nodded, smelling her scent on both.

"There's no necklace in here, and nothing is giving off enough of a signal to think it was spelled in any way," Roman mentioned as he emptied the space in the compartment under the stair and shut the lid.

"Do you have anything you want to tell us before we continue the search? Keep in mind, this is your chance to come clean before we find anything more incriminating than we already have," Ric warned.

The couple remained silent.

"I'll love every second of watching whatever punishment the Court finds appropriate for you," I quipped, passing them to follow Roman upstairs.

Roman mounted the steps and made his way down the hall, checking room by room. Still there was nothing.

"Anything?" I asked.

"I see what Kasun's saying about there being an imprint, but not having anything solid to go on. There's definitely something here, though."

Hope blossomed and began to take root.

Roman strode past me and just as I was about to turn and follow after him, something in my periphery caught my attention. Giving it a closer inspection, I saw the tiny end of a pull cord slipping out of a nearly invisible seam in the ceiling.

"Roman?"

"What?" he said, irritated.

"The ceiling. I think there's an attic up here." I pointed.

With a snap of his fingers, the panel swung down and produced a ladder to the space above.

"Now we're fucking talking," Roman said as he passed me and climbed up.

The attic was dusty and littered with boxes covered in illegible writing. As soon as I had completely entered the space, I could tell there was a very distinct shift in the air. There was something here that was lacking in the rest of the house, something begging to be discovered.

"Do you feel that?" I whispered, scanning the room.

"I do, but I didn't think your kind would," he remarked suspiciously.

"Normally, I wouldn't. I don't know how to explain it, but I can feel her close here."

Without saying another word, Roman strode forward, plowing through stacks of boxes. Glass cracking and heavy objects smacking the wooden floor filled my ears. That was going to suck for the unlucky son of a bitch cleaning this place.

Against the back wall, farthest from the trap door, sat an old wooden chest. It wasn't anything spectacular or something that particularly stood out, but there was an energy coming from it that couldn't be denied.

"Gentlemen, I think we may have struck gold here," Roman called over his shoulder, as he latched on to the box and dragged it out from where it sat.

Fuck! Mr. Grandville's thought came loud enough to stand out to me.

"I think you could be right, Roman. This one has loud thoughts about the box," I announced.

"Is that so?" Ric asked, eyes narrowed in the Grandvilles' direction.

Roman said a few unintelligible phrases as he focused on the lock. As soon as he finished, there was a loud click, just before the lock opened and fell to the floor with a hard metallic thud. The chest was dusty, but there were marks along the edges to suggest someone had messed with it recently.

Peering inside, I saw there were old pictures and folded materials that had to have been passed down for several generations. Shoving all of that aside, Roman uncovered a felt-encased jewelry box, made specifically to house a precious necklace. Not waiting another minute, he opened it, and lo and behold, Alina's opal necklace sat pristinely inside.

"Case closed, gentlemen," Roman muttered, handing the necklace over to me.

"Will you make this as simple as possible and let her out? I'll even throw you a bone and say please. Please?" I mocked, not expecting a damn thing from any of the witches.

As expected, Mr. and Mrs. Grandville leered defiantly at me as I handed it back over to Roman.

"Can you free her?" I asked, hoping like hell he had the ability to bring her out of wherever she was.

He nodded and took the opal from my hands. As soon as Roman's fingers brushed the opal, the air zinged to life, bursting with an electricity unlike I'd ever experienced. His focus was absolute, and the hairs along my arms and neck stood on end.

With a quick flip of his wrist, a bright white light exploded forth from the opal, blinding everyone who was watching. The glass in the window panes shook, yet there was no rumble through the house to cause such an effect. Without warning, Alina appeared, her back arching off the floor like she had been lifted. An anguished scream tore from her throat, and her eyes were black as tar. She began to speak in tongues none of us could understand.

"Roman? What the hell is going on?" I yelled, unable to look away from her.

Alina's veins were sticking out, and every muscle looked like it was stuck in mid-spasm. I spied Roman, whose concentration hadn't been broken by my question. His mouth barely moved, but I could hear his words. The lights along the walls grew brighter until I was sure they would blow the circuits. Just as suddenly, the lights dimmed to barely on, casting the room in darkness, and Alina fell to the floor with a thud before I could react and catch her.

"It's done," Roman announced with finality.

Alina was barely breathing, and I could hear the faint flutters of her heartbeat, but it wasn't strong, like it should have been. Ric took a step toward her, but I held a hand up. We didn't know what we were dealing with. I approached her carefully and kneeled down beside her shivering form. Her skin was slick with sweat and was growing pale compared to its usual tanned vibrancy. There was nothing that stood out to me as being wrong. Physically, she was fine. Mentally, she was confused, but that wasn't necessarily abnormal given her situation. There was a fear in her eyes that made my stomach drop to my toes. Whatever was ailing her was serious, and the only thing I could think of was the broken bond. The Grandvilles refused to release her from her confines, and the only way for her to be free was to the break the bond between her soul and the opal. Either way, one thing was becoming clearer by the second.

I was losing her.

Without thinking, I pushed up the sleeve of my dress shirt and homed in on the stark blue lines on my wrists, where my veins were. My fangs descended, and without wasting more time, I tore into my flesh before pushing it to her mouth.

"You need to drink, love. Trust me, everything is going to be all right. I promise," I whispered, letting her dark hair run through the fingers of my free hand.

Her mouth was slack at first, but then her lips closed over my skin. I felt her tongue caress the gash as my blood flowed into her. I watched her throat bob as she swallowed pull after pull. Gently, I pulled away from her. My flesh was already knitting itself back together while I held her and prayed for the best.

We were in uncharted territory.

CHAPTER 18

ALINA

I landed on my back, but I instantly knew something was wrong. It had to be. My magic hadn't come back, and my body was weak.

I didn't want to open my eyes, but there was an earsplitting ringing in my ears forcing me to search for the source. The light was too bright when I managed to crack an eye open. The room was crowded with people, some I knew and others who were total strangers to me.

All of the words were distorted and had echoes. My lips parted to say something, but my voice refused to cooperate.

Gabriel gathered my head onto his lap and kept his touch feather light. The hard wood floor grounded me to the present. It was so hard to focus on anything, and everything was too hazy. Something was definitely wrong with me. Fear crept in.

Gabriel's lips were moving and sounds were spilling from his handsome lips, but no matter how hard I tried to concentrate on what he was saying, I couldn't understand. The harder I tried to focus and make sense of things, the slipperier they became, always staying just out of my reach. My whole body felt floaty, almost as though if it weren't for Gabriel's hands acting as an anchor to the world, I'd lazily float away. Maybe I'd go somewhere in the beyond; I wasn't sure. The coppery tang of Gabriel's blood coated my mouth. I thought I'd be sick, but the spasms never came. I would've welcomed spasms. It would've been a sign of life, something that wasn't giving up. My reality was slipping away while I was incapable of doing a damn thing to stop it. Somewhere in the back of my mind, I knew I was fading into nothing. Being afraid would've been natural, but I didn't feel anything.

Darkness began to creep in around the edges of my vision. Breathing was hard; it felt like a horse was standing on my chest. My pulse pounded in my ears, slow enough that I saw the writing on the wall. I was dying.

Just as I thought my heart would stop forever, something changed. A subtle shift in my trajectory, as Gabriel's blood mingled with mine, healing every broken bit.

My heart began to beat stronger, and each breath came a little easier. The tiny flicker where my magic had been gave a small glimmer of hope as I felt it fanned back to life.

"Gabriel?" I whispered with more strength than I'd had before.

"I'm here."

I lifted my hand so he could see what I wanted to show him. My words were failing me, but he needed to know. Lifting my palm, I felt my magic flow freer than it ever had before and fill my palm. Without so much as an active thought, a small flame burst to life.

"We're going to be all right," I whispered, low enough so it could only be heard by his ears.

I gave him a weak smile before my eyes scanned the room, growing heavier by the second. A man and the one who'd broken the bond between my soul and the opal were escorting Mr. and Mrs. Grandville out of the room in handcuffs. Their children followed after one another, fear pooled in their eyes as they clung to each other.

I drifted off into the sweet oblivion of exhaustion, wondering what was to become of us all. However, that was a question for another day.

EPILOGUE

GABRIEL

The weeks following Alina's imprisonment were a whirlwind. The Court of the Sun and the Moon had convened to hand down punishment to the Grandvilles and determine the future of both myself and Alina here in Havenwood Falls.

The punishment for the Grandvilles was lacking. Alina wasn't of a similar mind on the subject. I wanted them to pay dearly, but Alina argued there were the children to take into account. Because the idea of owning Marid djinn, like her, had a long history which was deeply rooted in some, the Court found that while wrong, the Grandvilles hadn't really hurt Alina in any significant way.

They couldn't punish the *what if*.

Banishment was the final verdict. They left, the whole family, and had their memories wiped as they left the confines of the memory ward. There wasn't a day that went by that I didn't think about exacting revenge. But Alina needed me to be better than that.

Tabitha and Cornelius also had to be considered. The hatred and sense of entitlement found in their parents would likely grow to infect both of them. They weren't bad kids, and they didn't deserve the hand they'd been dealt.

Alina's father had finally called to congratulate her on making a life for herself. We managed to keep what had happened under wraps, though she did confess that she was now unemployed and depending on her boyfriend. Ignoring all the gory details, he wasn't thrilled, and he wanted to meet me right away.

Catching me staring at her from her periphery, she gave a sly smirk.

"What? Do I have something on my face?" Alina joked.

"No. Do I need a reason to admire you? To appreciate what a lucky son of a bitch I am that you chose me?" I teased, though there was nothing false in my confession.

"I suppose not, as long as you know just how lucky I am to be loved by someone like you. You never gave up on me, even when I'd just about given up on myself. You've stolen my heart and given me back my soul. Now that I know how sweet freedom truly tastes, I want to spend the rest of mine with you," she said with finality.

My hand slid from her lower back to the side of her neck, where I held her firmly. Swooping in, I stole a quick kiss. Her eyes reflected everything I was feeling.

Thanksgiving had passed, and now Christmas was coming in a few weeks, and there were some big things coming for us. In fact, we were on our way to the Court of the Sun and the Moon to petition them for my right to the vampire nest Viktor had once presided over.

With her hand wrapped securely in mine, we strolled down Eighth Street, admiring the glistening Christmas decorations the city had put up. Lighted snowflakes hung from street lamps, and the stores were beginning to put together their storefront holiday displays, making the picturesque town even more so. Almost losing Alina had put things into perspective and allowed me to appreciate the tiny in-between moments. Not just the major events, but the connecting time, when life really happened.

It had been three weeks, and I had yet to feel the urge to leave. Each day with her was a gift, one that I was beginning to see could last. I didn't even mind the stares we occasionally received. It was our own slice of normalcy, but first, we had one last hurdle.

Roman Bishop would be calling to cash in on that favor. When he would eventually call in his price, I'd pay it. I was a man of my word.

"Are you nervous?" she asked, tucking herself in closer.

"No. Nerves are for people who are unsure of themselves. I'm confident the Court will see that my claim is legitimate. I am Viktor's heir, and it's my duty to honor him as such. Besides, it's best to keep my kind on a tighter leash than most."

"I hope you're right. I love seeing you with such a purpose now. This is what you were always meant for, and I'm blessed to be by your side for this ride," she replied.

"I thank God every night for giving me the gift of dream walking. Without it, I never would've met you. I love you." I stopped and turned toward her, dipping down so I was level with her.

The ring in my pocket was heavy. When I took my place at the helm of the Lilith Nest, I'd ask her to rule by my side. It didn't matter that she was a djinn and the kindest person I'd ever met. She made me want to be better than the monster I'd been for so long.

"I love you too. Forever and always."

"Good. Now let's get to this hearing so I can get you home and out of that dress. I'm starving." I smirked.

Oh yes, it was going to be quite a night.

We hope you enjoyed this story in the Havenwood Falls series featuring a variety of supernatural creatures. The series is a collaborative effort by multiple authors.

Havenwood Falls books by Victoria Flynn:
Stolen Wishes
Sun & Moon Academy Book One: Fall Semester
Sun & Moon Academy Book Two: Spring Semester

Books in the Havenwood Falls Sin & Silk series:
Taming the Beast by Nadirah Foxx
Plans Laid Bare by JD Nelson
Shift of Fate by Victoria Escobar

Stolen Wishes by Victoria Flynn
Damned Allure by Justine Winter
Savage Salvation by Kristie Cook
Dark Seduction by Michele G. Miller & R.K. Ryals
Soul Laid Bare by JD Nelson
Stray With Me by E.J. Fechenda
Chase the Flames by Desiree Lafawn
Flirting With Death by Nadirah Foxx

Also try the signature line, Havenwood Falls, the historical paranormal line, Legends of Havenwood Falls, and stories from the local supernatural college in Sun & Moon Academy.

Stay up to date at www.HavenwoodFalls.com

Subscribe to our reader group and receive free stories and more!

ABOUT THE AUTHOR

Victoria Flynn is a married mother to two daughters. She loves to travel and try new things and experiences, and spending time with friends and family. Her favorite place in the entire world is New Orleans, including everything from the mudbugs to the swamps, and yes, even a HUGE ASS BEER. When she's not writing, she can be found with her nose buried in a good book or outside enjoying the unpredictable Michigan weather. Victoria graduated from the University of Michigan with a degree in Biology and published her first novel, *A Soul's Sacrifice*, her senior year in between classes and homework. She loves the paranormal and loves to explore historical places, hopefully combining the two.

ACKNOWLEDGMENTS

First and foremost, I would like to thank Kristie Cook for being a fabulous editor and for giving me the opportunity to share a part of this world. You have pushed me to become a better writer, and I thank you for it. To Regina Wamba, your work on the cover still amazes me, and I'm honored to provide a story that showcases your work. This book wouldn't have been possible without the help of the Havenwood Falls authors, all of whom offered advice and coached me when it came to crossover characters. To my husband, Jacob, thank you for never letting me quit even when I'm crying and sure the end of my writing career is knocking on the door. You believe in me even when I don't believe in myself.

AN EXCERPT

Damned Allure (A Havenwood Falls Sin & Silk Novella) by Justine Winter

What do you do when Death's hot on your heels for messing with the afterlife order?

Yeah, I'm a smooth guy, generally. But some damned souls escaped the Infernum during my last visit, and now I'm Death's chew toy. I've gotta track and return these supernatural fugitives before they cause more carnage. Easy, right? Except Nyx, a vampire-demon hybrid, is leading these already corrupt souls astray and turning a secret town upside down during her pursuit for queendom of the Underworld. Crazy bitches come with crazy ideas.

I arrive in Havenwood Falls in the midst and madness of a Hot Cocoa and Cookie Crawl. I don't expect to be swallowed up by this mystical town with its own enchantments, luring me in with its hidden beauty. There are secrets much deeper than what appears on the surface. One in particular has sinful legs and silky hair I'm desperate to bury myself into. She's hooked me like a gullible puppy owner, trapped by those stunning eyes. I'm screwed. Literally.

Sadly, Death is still snapping at my ass, halting my attempts to unravel this beauty's darkest desires. The Infernum demands Nyx's soul be amongst the others to be returned, and I *will* reap them. I am their courier to Hell.

My name is Shade StormIron, and I am an Angel of Death.

DAMNED ALLURE

"Fuck me, you're a feisty one, aren't you? Don't you wanna play nice for Big Daddy?" I tease the bitch trying to wriggle free from my arm. She's a fighter, I'll give her that. I tighten my hold as we descend from the inky night sky, swirling like wisps of black smoke until we breach the realm boundaries to the Infernum.

"Take. Me. Back!" She huffs out every syllable, straining as she tries to halt my progress, using what strength and weight she has left to keep me from depositing her damned soul into Hell's special holding place. These buggers never think they'll be caught and end up here. It's fucking hilarious really—where else do they think their death will send them? Supernatural creatures are my worst clients, reckoning they can screw the world over and not be punished for it. Stupid bastards.

"Cut this shit out, or I'll make sure your time in the Infernum is as painful and torturous as possible."

She tuts. "You don't have that kind of power. You're just a messenger boy."

She laughs maniacally as though the fringe of the Infernum's entrance is already driving her crazy.

Screams and howls pierce the atmosphere; the walls bleed misery and torment, a promise of suffering for all trapped here. There's no escaping now.

I let her go, knowing her soul is now anchored to the Infernum's clutches.

"I may be Death's bitch," I begin, taking a cursory glance around the area. Fire and brimstone burst through cracks in this sweat box, and sulfur permeates the charred air. It's bloody offensive to my senses, like some inconsiderate arsehole's left a dead animal to rot in the scorching sun. The only thing missing here is the blowflies to gorge on these corpses. "But at least I don't have to spend an eternity listening to these acoustics and smelling shit all day. Have fun, bitch!"

I turn and walk away, releasing any hidden ties I still have on her. I meant it before—I'm not bound for an existence here. I'm an approved visitor only. These evil motherfucking souls are not bringing me down with them.

A loud whistle cuts through the oppressive air. "I see you're still making friends. You ever try bringing someone in without pissing them off, Shade?"

"What fun would that be?" I let a cheeky smile cover my face, though it's somewhat difficult to see when my face lacks flesh. Really, I'm just showing off a perfect set of teeth all denture-wearing oldies are jealous of. I'm still the sexiest skeleton around. I've got big bones, if you know what I mean. "Nobody ever wants to come down here willingly. You were the same, Sapphire. I almost broke a nail delivering you."

"You'd need nails first, Shade. Have you missed me?" The vampire sulks toward me, reaching out to touch my chest cavity.

"Babe, you might have been smokin' hot up top on Earth, but down here your skin looks like it's been ravished by moths. You're holier than all the angels." I roar with laughter, momentarily silencing the usual musical screams.

"At least I've still got skin." She pushes away from me, taking any more thoughts of seduction with her. Thank fuck. One more year down here and a human corpse will be fresher than this stubborn supernatural stiff. There's no talent for beauty contests down here.

"Sapphire, before you go, there's something you forgot," I call out, smirking to myself.

"You're not getting a kiss, Shade. Please yourself," she replies over her shoulder, not daring to look my way.

"Oh, I will, but really, you forgot something . . ." I wait until she gives in, striding with purpose to me. Her eyes widen as she catches sight of my bony hands holding something she wants back. I flex my fingers over the mass.

"What are you doing?" She seems horrified, which is quite impressive considering her home is the Infernum.

"I told you, you forgot something."

"I see that." She grits her teeth. "But what are you *doing* to it?"

"Chill, babe. I'm just squeezing a piece of your arse."

Fucking priceless.

"You finished torturing us poor souls yet?"

I stop when I hear the deep timbre of an old acquaintance. I lean against a sweat-dripping wall, crossing my skeletonized arms over my chest, my hooded black cloak flowing freely around me. I'm a handsome bastard, really.

"You ever had a woman fall apart in front of you, my friend?" I ask.

"We both know I don't do emotions, Shade." Jax, a long-serving Infernum inmate, speaks.

I shake my head. "I mean literally. That shit is hilarious." I laugh out loud all over again. The old vamp's face had been quite the picture of horror. Talk about embarrassing. "She put her arse right in my hands. Don't get more forward than that."

We giggle like a pair of schoolgirls.

"Man, this place fucks you up for good." Jax shakes his head, and I realize how tired the old bear shifter looks. Amazingly, he's endured the Infernum for a century already, and considering how slow time moves here, that's a feat in itself. Most souls crumble after five minutes because it seems like five *decades* have already passed.

"You coping? You're looking uglier these days," I quip, remembering the youthful shifter all those years ago.

"Speak for yourself, mate. Did you lose weight? You're looking gaunt."

If I had organs they'd be falling out of me with the vibrations of my laughter ripping through me.

"Dude, whatever it is you're doing to keep that humor of yours going, promise me you'll keep the secret to yourself. Otherwise, next time I drop in, I'm gonna have a riot on my hands. Anyway, gotta fly. I can hear my theme tune playing." I motion to my skull, referring to the sound of another soul that needs reaping. Death's a greedy bugger, never satisfied.

A shiver runs along my spine like fine hairs tickling my weathered bones. The air compresses around me, squeezing until I become a swirl of black mist again, my wings flapping eagerly.

I zip around the Infernum, missing walls and dodging streams of lava as I break the speed barriers whilst ascending with purpose, leaving the bleak abyss behind.

This place is no holiday destination.

A high-pitched squeal cripples my wings, and I fall, clutching the sides of my skull as pain radiates all over. I forget my flight, the urge to answer a soul's calling taking a back seat. I can't think through the agony the squeals bring. It's like my bones are being pulverized, one small section at a time as though to prolong my despair.

I'm barely aware of how fast I'm falling, how quickly fire and stone walls are now looming over me.

I pull at my skull, desperate to keep the noise from assaulting me further. My efforts bring zero comfort. It's futile, and yet, like a fucking idiot, I can't stop searching for a reprieve, like a magical mute button's going to appear on my cranium.

A sense of foreboding engulfs every inch of me, like darkness is claiming me.

"Shit!" I smack the ground with such force, it's inadvertently become my submissive. On the plus side, the pain's gone, but that's only because I've become completely numb. I'm like a Halloween pinup. Tape me to the front door, and I'll rattle the window in the wind, swinging to and fro like a puppet without strings.

"How nice it is to see you, Shade."

Shit, I inwardly groan. "Well, you know, I thought it was about time I drop in to see the big boss." I keep my distance from the tall entity in front of me.

"Don't bullshit me. Your worthiness is on the line."

I gulp, keeping my mouth shut for fear I'll say something stupid, like another pun that goes unnoticed.

"You fucked up good." Death's dark stare drives fear into my essence. I can feel terror imprinting on my bones. The otherworldly being is like a giant in size and always has his skeletal frame smartly dressed in an array of tailored suits. Besides his height, I'm sure shopping for such clothing is pretty easy. After all, he's never gonna be more than a size zero. Catwalk models would envy our figures—I hear stick-thin is in this season.

At this moment, Death's wearing his favorite onyx suit, as he likes to call it. Honestly, I don't get the bloody color names myself. I see no difference in tones. Black is black, no matter its sale-savvy description. And don't even get me started on the stupid thorned stem he's got peeking out of his pocket. There's no flower head, of course. Nothing can live with Death around. Literally. He really brings out the lack of life in the room.

Shit, he's crossed his bones over his chest, squaring shoulders he doesn't have—the suit does the work for him.

"You don't have anything to tell me? Some remorse perhaps?"

At what point am I supposed to blow his anger up by saying I don't understand to what he's referring?

Oh bollocks, I'm going to cease to exist.

"How many imbeciles do I have to employ to collect souls and get the job done? It's not fucking difficult!" Death roars, temper raging as he kicks out at the tall stands holding flames that illuminate the otherwise dark space. Fire scatters on the concrete ground, burning everything in its path, including my feet. It's a good thing I don't have any skin.

"Dude, you need to tone it down. I've been reaping souls perfectly. In fact, I just dropped another into the Infernum."

Death leans down, putting his hand in front of me. It's as large as my body. With finger and thumb he flicks me hard, sending me across the room until I hit a wall that stops me.

"Don't you fucking 'dude' me, arsehole. This is my place you're fucking with." He stomps toward me. Two steps is all it takes for him to lift me until his large skull is in front of me, mouth opening as though he's going to eat me. I don't know why—the only thing I'm good for is picking meat out of his teeth *after* dinner. "You allowed some souls to escape the goddamn Infernum!"

Death's breath wafts in my face like a gale-force wind. Shit, pass the dead guy a breath mint; he smells worse than a sewer.

"When?" I can't help the shock creeping into my voice. This is news to me. Wouldn't I know if someone left the Infernum? Despite the fact it's bloody impossible in the first place. This has to be some lame joke he's trying to pull on me—the big guy never can match my comedy.

"Not ten minutes ago. While you were busy chatting with our long-term patrons, they were distracting you from the miscreants using the portal you opened to get there. Now they're running free again. Only this time with even less of a conscience." Death's hand smacks me across the other side of the room. I struggle to stand, mostly out of fear of being flung around the room again. This shit hurts.

Did the bear shifter really sell me out? Sapphire I can understand. That bitch always has something brewing in her conniving mind. It's what sent her into the pits of the Infernum in the first place.

"I'll bring them back," I vow, slowly rising to my feet like a beaten man. When Death hits you, you know you're going down for good.

"You'd fucking better, especially the one that orchestrated this whole plan." Though he doesn't have any eyebrows, I imagine Death's scowling at me right now. The dark abyss of his eyes promises loneliness and pain if I fail to deliver.

I try straightening my cloak, brushing off the dust and flames I picked up from my acquaintance with the ground.

"Just out of curiosity, who's the evil mastermind behind all of this?"

Death smiles widely, leaning back into the throne he spends most of his time in. "Nyx, the vampire-demon hybrid. Bring them all back before they cause even more damage to the world."

I nod, knowing I have a lot of work on my hands—Nyx had been tough to capture the first time. I turn, opening up a new portal, where it will lead me to a damned soul's location. As a reaper, it's like I have my own tracking system—the souls call to me whether they know it or not.

"Oh, and Shade, one last thing. If you fuck this up even more, and fail to deliver Nyx to me personally, you're done. No more privileges. No more slack. No more wings. I'll disintegrate your existence."

I close my eyes, taking in the severity of the situation. Just as I step into the portal, I hear Death chuckle. "Good luck!"

Purchase *Damned Allure* where books are sold.